"Wel___ to Me___ ___'s
Trendy ___ ___ ___ ___ ___ the
cleverly desig___ ___ ___ ___ 'll soon
be yearning fo___ ___ ___ ___ izzy; her best
friend, Rena; and ___ ___ and Jinx. Annie Knox
has created a war___ ___ flawed, but completely en-
dearing sleuth in ___ McHale, and I'm already panting for the next book in the series."

—Miranda James, *New York Times* bestselling
author of the Cat in the Stacks mysteries

"Five paws up! Annie Knox dazzles with four-legged
friends, fashion, and foul play. *Paws for Murder* is tai-
lor-made for the pet and mystery lover."

—Melissa Bourbon, national bestselling author of
A Seamless Murder

"Everything you could hope for in a good cozy. . . . I
spent the duration of the tale dying to know what happens next, yet simultaneously wanting to savor every
word. The story is swiftly paced, the plot is tightly wo-
ven, and the mystery's a real head scratcher."

—*Crimespree Magazine*

"A witty whodunit . . . one that fans of corpses and
canines, felonies and felines, will lap up."

—*Richmond Times-Dispatch*

"A winning mystery series that will keep you enter-
tained until the very end." —Books-n-Kisses

continued . . .

Also by Wendy Watson Writing as Annie Knox

Pet Boutique Mysteries

Paws for Murder
Groomed for Murder

By Wendy Watson

Mystery à la Mode Mysteries

I Scream, You Scream
Scoop to Kill
A Parfait Murder

Collared for Murder

A PET
BOUTIQUE MYSTERY

Annie Knox

OBSIDIAN
Published by the Penguin Group
Penguin Group (USA) LLC, 375 Hudson Street,
New York, New York 10014

USA | Canada | UK | Ireland | Australia | New Zealand | India | South Africa | China
penguin.com
A Penguin Random House Company

First published by Obsidian, an imprint of New American Library,
a division of Penguin Group (USA) LLC

First Printing, June 2015

ISBN 978-0-451-24113-9

Printed in the United States of America
10   9   8   7   6   5   4   3   2   1

PUBLISHER'S NOTE
This is a work of fiction. Names, characters, places, and incidents either are
the product of the author's imagination or are used fictitiously, and any re-
semblance to actual persons, living or dead, business establishments, events,
or locales is entirely coincidental.

    The recipes contained in this book are to be followed exactly as written.
The publisher is not responsible for your specific health or allergy needs that
may require medical supervision. The publisher is not responsible for any
adverse reactions to the recipes contained in this book.

For Todd. You were an inspiration to us all.

Acknowledgments

As always, this book wouldn't have been possible without the village of readers, friends, experts, and editors who have helped me along the way. A special thank-you to Dean James for being such a tremendous support to me over the years. Becky Galloway provided invaluable insight into the world of cat shows; any errors in their depiction are purely my own. Sandy Harding is simply the best editor I could hope for, providing just the right balance of encouragement and independence. Finally, I would like to thank my tremendous copy editor, whose attention to detail humbles me.

CHAPTER
One

Dee Dee Lahti stood in the middle of Ballroom One at the North Woods Hotel, her aqua kaftan billowing in the intermittent wind from an oscillating fan, a patient Maine coon hanging from her hands by his armpits. She cocked her frizzy head, scanning the hutches and velvet-draped cages lining the benches. Her mouth—generously outlined in mauve—moved softly as she maintained a running conversation with herself.

Without warning, she lurched forward and down, as though she were falling, and began to shove the cat into a pink leopard-print and PVC hutch.

Pamela Rawlins had been chatting idly with me as I arranged my chiffon ruffs, hand-wrought collar dangles, and delicate clips sporting rhinestones, bows, and small beaded flowers on my vendor's table. When Dee Dee crammed that cat into the hutch, though, she stiffened and sucked in a breath, her patrician nostrils pinching shut. "I swear, that woman has less sense than a box of hair," she muttered.

"Dee Dee, darling," she called. "You really must put the correct cat in the correct enclosure." She bit off her words like a Connecticut blue blood. Or a shark.

Dee Dee looked up, her features scrunched in confusion.

"You can't put Phantom in Charleston's hutch."

Dee Dee stared at the cat she had just deposited and then leaned in to look at the picture pinned to the outside of the enclosure. She stood straight and looked back at us, her expressive face slack, blank.

"You just put Phantom in Charleston's hutch. Phantom should be in his *own* enclosure." Nothing. "The cage with the red velvet drape."

"Are you sure?" Dee Dee said.

Pamela took a beat. "Of course I'm sure, you . . ." She didn't finish the sentence, but even Dee Dee knew where she was going.

Pamela was correct that Dee Dee Lahti was a few walleye short of a fish fry. Still, the residents of Merryville were one big dysfunctional family. We could harbor grudges against one another, whisper spiteful things behind one another's backs, and, yes, even occasionally call Dee Dee Lahti "dingbat." To her face.

But Pamela wasn't part of the family, and I felt a surge of protectiveness when she sniped at poor Dee Dee.

I'd seen Phantom and Charleston, both silver-and-white Maine coons. "Pamela," I said, "it's an easy mistake to make. The cats are almost identical."

Pamela angled her body to face me, her small birdlike eyes utterly flat and emotionless. "I'm aware of that, Ms. McHale. *Almost* identical but not *actually* identical. If she can't tell the difference between those silver markings, how will she tell the difference between two lilac-point Himalayans?"

I raised my chin a notch.

She allowed herself a tight shake of her head. "This is all highly irregular. I told Marsha Denford that we shouldn't vary from our usual procedures. The annual retreat for the Midwestern Cat Fanciers' Organization has a pristine reputation precisely because we have rules and we follow them to the letter. Our silver anniversary is not the time to start bending those rules."

I'd heard this argument a good dozen times since the M-CFO had decided to host their twenty-fifth annual retreat in our little town. Marsha Denford, wife of the organization's president, Phillip Denford, had taken a shine to Pris Olson, owner of Prissy's Pretty Pets. While the official rules of the organization specified that the cats were not to be handled by anyone other than the owners and the judges, Marsha had arranged for Pris to provide grooming services in the back corner of the ballroom, right next to the service entrance. Pris had a crackerjack crew of groomers, but she'd taken pity on Dee Dee Lahti—who was unemployed and in constant misery, thanks to her habitual criminal of a husband—by allowing her to help out. Dee Dee was not crackerjack.

Apparently sensing tension in the air, Pris left off supervising her employees and floated our way. "Pamela. Izzy. Is there a problem?" she cooed. Pris sported a perfectly painted beauty-pageant smile and a practiced, formal politeness that screamed privilege.

"Practiced" is the key word here. In public Pris defined "Minnesota nice." The term refers to the smiling openness and back-bending helpfulness that most Minnesotans seemed to exude from birth. Sometimes Minnesota nice was genuine. Sometimes it was not.

I knew firsthand that Pris's brilliant white smile could be a trap, a colorful Amazonian flower that promised sweet nectar before clamping shut around some poor, unsuspecting insect.

No one was safe. We were all insects in Pris's world.

Now Pris and Pamela faced each other like a photograph and its negative: both tall, elegantly slim, hair pulled back in a sleek knot, clad in figure-skimming suits. But where Pris wore baby pink that matched the soft blush of her porcelain skin, her eyes a pale Nordic blue, her hair shining the color of fresh butter, Pamela's olive complexion reflected the onyx black of her hair, eyes, and suit.

I took a step back. Like all the McHale sisters, I'm tall and athletic. In theory, I could snap either one of these model-thin women in half. In a physical fight, I had them licked. But this promised to be another round in the women's months-long battle of wills, and I was hopelessly outmatched.

Pamela's crimson mouth oozed into a smile. "Mrs. Olson—"

"Please, call me Pris."

A heartbeat of silence.

"Pris, your assistant over there"—she waved dismissively in Dee Dee's general direction—"was just returning Phantom to Charleston's hutch."

"Oh dear," Pris gushed. "Well, those two big boys really do look alike. And I did urge Mrs. McCoy to stay with us while we gave Phantom his blowout. It's our policy, you know. But she was far too eager to start catching up with the other breeders, so she left Phantom on his own. I'm sure she didn't even consider the possibility that her cat would be confused for another, nearly identical cat, but that's what policies are for!" Pris concluded, her mouth settling into a wicked little smile.

Harsh red heat roiled across Pamela's cheeks. I took another step back. Pamela was about to blow.

Still, when she rallied enough to speak, her voice

remained as flat as Iowa. "You're absolutely correct. That's why we have policies. Like the policy of requiring owners to groom their own animals."

Pris raised a single shoulder. "Well. What are you gonna do?"

The phrase was as much challenge as expression of commiseration.

I held my breath, waiting for the fireworks, but they never came; the whole situation defused when my aunt Dolly sashayed up, back from her tour around the ballroom. In typical Dolly style, she wore glittering stack-heeled sandals. Her tunic-length T-shirt, featuring a tropical sunset picked out in sequins, draped over a pair of neon-orange capris. No matter the occasion, Dolly dressed with flair.

"Ladies," she drawled, head swiveling back and forth between Pris and Pamela like she was watching a match at Wimbledon.

"Hello, Dolly," Pris responded.

Pamela extended a hand. "I don't think I've had the pleasure."

My aunt took the proffered hand and gave it two vigorous shakes. "My name is Dolly," she said, overenunciating each word. "Just like Pris said," she added helpfully.

The tendons in Pamela's neck stood out. "I'm Pamela Rawlins, cocoordinator of the show."

Dolly grinned. "Well, it's a mighty fine cat show.

Not that I've ever been to a cat show before. But this is terrific. I've never seen so much drama packed into a single room.

"That lady over there," she said, jerking her thumb in the direction of a heavyset woman in a cobalt-blue tracksuit, "said that sometimes people poison other people's cats." She shivered in morbid delight.

I gasped. "Really?" I said, turning to Pamela for verification.

"Once," she said emphatically. "That was six years ago. And the accused insists to this day she accidentally dropped those acetaminophen tablets into Betsy Blue's bowl of kibble. Besides, she's been permanently banned from participating in our shows."

I was still reeling from the notion that a cat owner would poison someone else's pet when Dolly jumped in again.

"That guy over in the corner," she said, indicating a balding gentleman wearing an Argyle sweater-vest despite the summer heat. He glanced up, almost as though he knew we were talking about him, but then went back to methodically running a brush over the sleek coat of a caramel-colored Burmese. "He confided that one of the female judges slipped her room key under Toffee Boy"—which must have been the cat—"when she returned him to his cage."

Pamela appeared stricken. "That doesn't happen anymore."

"Ha! He said it happened last year."

Pamela quirked her head to the side, frowning in confusion. Her eyes scanned the room, pausing on each judging ring. Her lips moved slightly as she counted them off.

"Well," she finally said, "I assure you that I run a tight ship. There will be no such shenanigans under my watch."

Dolly shook her head. "I hate to tell you, Ms. Pamela Rawlins, but I have a hunch that this week will be a hotbed of shenanigans. And my hunches are never wrong."

"Are we ready?" Rena asked.

"I don't know. Are we?" I countered.

Rena Hamilton had been my best friend since grade school. We made an unlikely pair. I was tall, clocking in at five foot ten inches when I slumped, dressed like the small-town girl that I was, and rarely made waves. Rena, on the other hand, was a giant personality in an elfin package. She'd toned herself down for the cat show, hoping she wouldn't scare away the out-of-town guests: she'd removed most of her piercings, all tattoos were covered, she'd put away every piece of spiked jewelry, and the knee-high Doc Martens were resting comfortably at home. Still, she couldn't do much to hide her Day-Glo-orange shock of hair or the gritty determination in her eyes.

In addition to the bond of friendship, we shared ownership of Trendy Tails. I ran the pet-boutique part of our shop, designing and hand making many of our wares, while Rena baked organic pet treats for our barkery and helped me with inventory, accounting, and manning the showroom.

"I've got the goodies and the doohickey that will let us process credit cards with your phone," she said.

"And I've got the merch and the change for cash purchases."

"Then I guess we're as ready as we'll ever be. All we'll need is some hot coffee to hit the ground running in the morning."

She paused to scan the ballroom of the North Woods Hotel, where, in a few short hours, the M-CFO show would kick off. At that point, the perimeter of the ballroom had been divided into cubbies—most of them rings in which cats would actually be judged, but a few, like ours, dedicated to cat-related vendors. The center of the floor was lined with rows of tables on which competitors had set up hutches for the show cats and a few for cats available for sale or adoption. While we watched, the cat owners and breeders were busy setting up their stations, and a dozen show volunteers were flitting about with clipboards and harried expressions.

"How have things been going here in the heart of the action?" Rena asked.

"Pamela is being a witch with a capital B. Dolly's been working the crowd for gossip and information on the salacious underbelly of cat shows. And one of the breeders lost her cool when someone said her tabby's scarab marking looked a little muddled."

"Scarab?"

"That sort of triangular marking right on the top of tabbies' heads. It's supposed to be clearly defined."

"Who knew?"

I laughed. "I sure didn't. But the breeder, that woman with the leopard-print jumpsuit, about blew a gasket when the dude in the plaid jacket mentioned it."

"The show's very first catfight?" Rena looked at me with wide-eyed innocence.

Before I could call her on her terrible joke, a sharp "no" brought all the conversation in the North Woods Hotel Ballroom One to a sudden halt. Every head swiveled to the source of the sound—Pris Olson, standing in front of Phillip Denford, both of them smack in the middle of the ballroom.

Denford was rocking back on his heels, his hands clasped behind his back and a smug smile on his face. He was the calm in the storm of Pris's ire. Denford looked every inch the man of leisure, his salt-and-pepper hair perfectly groomed and his loosely knotted tie and perfectly pressed chinos conveying that he was absolutely in charge but that he carried the burden with ease. Phillip Denford was the spectacularly wealthy head of the Midwestern Cat Fanciers' Organization and the person footing the bill for much of the week's activities. He'd first made a fortune in business real estate and venture capitalism, and then he'd doubled down by opening the Web's two most well-known sites for upscale pet products: the Dapper Dog and the Classy Cat. Denford was too important, both because of his money and because of his sway in the world of cat fanciers and canine aficionados, for anyone to call him out for his loathsome ways, but the word "letch" had been carried by a constant flurry of whispers ever since he'd arrived. Even as he and Pris argued, his eyes weren't exactly glued to her face.

Pris generally respected wealth and power, and after years of marriage to the Midwest's RV King, she knew how to deal with men who had wandering eyes and wayward hands. More important, she certainly wanted to stay in Denford's good graces. Befriending anyone with money and connections offered Pris an opportunity to advance her own interests. But something he'd said or done had pushed her over the edge. I couldn't begin to imagine what.

Pris leaned in to give Phillip what for. Even angry, Pris managed to be gorgeous. You could tell she was royally po'd by her expression, but her face didn't get that mottled red color mine did when I was angry.

No, Pris's cheeks just got a little rosier. I'm not usually one to get hung up on looks, but I'll admit I resented her unfaltering beauty just a bit.

After that initial outburst, I couldn't hear what Pris was saying, but she continued to stab at Phillip's chest with her finger.

"Poor Pris," I muttered.

Rena Hamilton twitched her nose. "What do you mean 'Poor Pris'?" Her contempt for Pris Olson dripped like venom from her every word. "Pris doesn't need your sympathy, Izzy. She's a rich, beautiful, successful queen bee of the Methodist Ladies' Auxiliary . . ."

". . . hates her husband, has recently lost a major chunk of her fortune, and is now enduring Phillip Denford's ogling."

Rena snorted. "First, it's Hal Olson's own fault he lost so much money. He sank way too much cash into the Badger Lake condos."

It was true. Hal had purchased a huge plot of land on the shores of Badger Lake and had begun building luxury condos for Merryville's many vacationers. It was an expensive proposition, but he'd planned to pay off the builders with income from the first few sales. Then, however, he ran afoul of the Department of Natural Resources because his building threatened the habitat of some endangered burrowing owls. As a result, he couldn't sell the condos yet, and the builders were starting to slap him with mechanics' liens. If he didn't reach some settlement with the DNR or start selling other assets, he'd risk his builders foreclosing on the property altogether.

I hummed my assent. "But it's not his fault that that new RV lot opened up down near the Cities, cutting into his business. And even if Hal's financial woes *are* his own fault, Pris is the one who's paying for them. She's been working extra shifts at Prissy's Pretty Pets. I mean actually working, ruining her manicures with doggy shampoo and getting clawed when the cats object to having their nails trimmed."

"Cry me a river."

"She's started selling scented candles and dietary supplements to the other ladies who live out in Quail Run. Dru told me she even had some sort of jewelry party. Mix-and-match charm bracelets of some sort."

"And what's the matter with hustling a little to bring home the bacon?" Rena sniffed as she straightened a display of custom-embroidered collars. Rena had been hustling to feed herself and her alcoholic father since she was fifteen.

"Nothing. Nothing at all. Except I hear no one is buying. All those so-called friends of hers are letting her go through her whole spiel about enhanced metabolism or the importance of aromatherapy or whatever, and then they smile, say no, and show her the door. It must be so embarrassing for her."

Unmoved, Rena brushed a smudge of powdered

sugar off her sleeve. Apparently, she'd had doughnuts for breakfast. "Why do you care? Pris is generally horrible to you. Maybe this is just a little karma."

I shrugged. "I just feel sorry for her."

"You know that she would kill you if you said that to her." Rena laughed.

I chuckled. "Oh yes. I know."

We turned back to see whether Denford and Pris were still bickering. Sure enough, Pris had managed to inch forward until her face was so close to Denford's that they almost seemed intimate.

I glanced around the room. Off by the sixth judging ring, Phillip's wife stood next to a slouchy, surly young man and watched the drama unfold. Marsha was a lovely woman, with long auburn hair, luscious curves, and eyes as blue as a winter sky, but she was wifty. Her voice trailed off at the end of every sentence, as though her thoughts were as ephemeral as dandelion fluff. She watched Phillip and Pris with her perpetual half smile on her face. Whatever transpired between her husband and the gorgeous blonde, Marsha remained unruffled.

"Who's the guy next to Marsha Denford? She's practically falling on top of him," I asked Rena.

She craned her head to see over all the kennels and snorted. "Marsha may be slightly inebriated. I think she'd hang on to anyone in her orbit, but that happens to be the younger Denford, Phillip's son by his first wife. His name is Peter."

"What's his story? Why on earth is he here?"

"He's an artist," Rena scoffed—a strange reaction since Rena's girlfriend, Jolly, was a jeweler and I, too, considered myself something of an artist when I designed my clothes for critters.

I gave Peter a closer look: a paper cup of coffee that probably cost him four dollars, a collarless linen shirt, well-worn cargo pants, Teva-like sandals, a fringed scarf looped around his neck, and a shock of red-gold hair with that messy look that can be achieved only with an array of expensive styling products.

So he was that kind of artist. The kind of artist who sneered a lot.

Sure enough, that's exactly what he was doing as he watched Pris and his dad squabble: he was sneering.

"As to why he's here," Rena continued, "I understand that he doesn't have many resources of his own. If you want to eat from the gravy train, you apparently have to follow it all around the Upper Midwest."

"Quite a family," I muttered.

"Which family?" The familiar deep voice behind me made me go a little gooey inside. "Yours? What have they been up to now?" Jack Collins, my boyfriend, was the only child of conventional parents. He

understood crazy—he was a cop. But the affable snip-
ing of the McHale sisters, my mother's stoic effort to
act like we were all angels, and my aunt Dolly's complete lack of self-control bemused him.

"Actually, the Denfords," I said as I turned to greet
him. He was holding a giant bouquet of balloons in
his giant fist, all bright green and baby blue—the Trendy
Tails colors. I gasped.

He tilted his close-cropped blond head, his eyes
alight with smug self-satisfaction, and offered the ribbons to me. "I thought they'd give your table some
height, make sure people can see you from clear across
the room."

"Brilliant! They're perfect." I dipped my chin and
looked up at him through my lashes. "And so are you,"
I said softly, for his ears alone.

"Most girls would hold out for diamonds before
they dished out that kind of praise. If I'd known a
handful of balloons would do the trick, I would have
been bringing them to your doorstep every day."

As I took the balloons, I realized they were actually
separated into two bouquets, each attached to a solid
weight that would keep them on our table. I handed
one of them off to Rena for the far end of the table and
placed mine right in the middle of a display of silk-
flower hair accessories.

I wrapped my arms around Jack in an impulsive
hug, and he leaned in to brush a kiss across my cheek.

We both pulled back with blushes starting to creep up our faces. We'd been dating for several months, but we were taking it slowly. My ill-fated engagement to my high school sweetheart had left me love-shy, and Jack honored that. Perhaps even more important, public displays of affection meant that, if the relationship went south, it would do so publicly, and after my debacle with Casey Alter, another public breakup was the last thing I wanted.

Jack cleared his throat as he put a few more inches of distance between us. "The Denfords, huh? From what little I've seen, they're proof that money can't ward off the crazies. Got a call down to the Silent Woman last night that that Peter kid was causing a ruckus. Kept calling himself a poor little rich boy and wouldn't pay his tab. Since the patrol guys were all out on more urgent calls, I decided to handle the call myself."

"Did you arrest him?"

"No."

"Really? That seems so unlike you." Jack had little patience for drunken foolishness, and I would have expected him to haul young Peter out by the ear and toss him in the drunk tank.

He shrugged. "By the time I got there, he'd called his dad's assistant to bail him out, pay his tab, and give him a ride home."

"Still doesn't sound like you, Mr. Law and Order,"

I teased. "Wouldn't expect you to let a rabble-rouser walk just because he had a ride home."

He looked down and stubbed his toe into the low-pile carpet. "It was a personal favor."

I couldn't imagine that Jack Collins and Peter Denford had ever crossed paths, so Jack's favor must have been for the rescuer, Phillip Denford's assistant. Curious.

A resounding "You!" from the center of the ballroom signaled that Phillip and Pris were still going at it. "That," I said, jerking my head in their direction, "is what got us talking about the Denfords."

"What's the fight about?" Jack asked.

"Don't know," Rena answered.

As we rubbernecked, a tiny wisp of a woman darted into the center of the fight. She had an abundance of curly blond hair piled on top of her head in a messy bun and a cherub's face. She wore a T-shirt with the Midwestern Cat Fanciers' Organization logo across the front and a pair of low-slung skinny jeans.

She rested a hand on Phillip's arm and the other on Pris's arm, looking back and forth between the two with an earnest expression.

"Who's that?" Rena asked.

"Marigold Aames," Jack and I said simultaneously. I shot him a surprised look, but he just shrugged.

"And she is . . . ?" Rena continued.

"She's Phillip's assistant. Pamela Rawlins is technically in charge of this shindig, but Marigold has done most of the heavy lifting. Pamela is in charge of the cat show, but Marigold has handled the extravaganza: the closing-night masquerade, the flowers and luncheons, the vendor space."

We all watched as Marigold shifted both hands to Pris's arm and guided her toward the door—toward us. At first Marigold's head nodded softly as Pris continued to gesticulate. Finally, Marigold said something, and Pris pulled her arm away. As Pris stalked toward us, Marigold took two skipping steps to every one of Pris's strides. It looked like Marigold was still trying to smooth the waters, but Pris's face was set in rigid determination. Just as the two got to our table, Marigold stopped, her shoulders slumped, while Pris continued out the door without a word.

Marigold ran a hand over her face and visibly shook off the tension of the moment. Then she caught sight of our little gaggle, and an enormous smile wreathed her face. "Jack!"

"Hi, Mari," he responded with a big grin.

She launched herself at him, and he caught her up in a big bear hug. Rena and I exchanged questioning looks.

"Izzy, Rena, this is Mari Aames. We went to college together at UMD."

"We were . . . great friends," Mari added, a faint splash of color on her cheeks.

My mind was whirling. Marigold had all but announced that she and Jack had been romantically involved. I knew that Jack had dated a girl named Jenny in college. They'd actually been engaged for a while. But it had never occurred to me that he might have had other significant relationships. He'd never mentioned Mari. *Why* had he never mentioned Mari?

And Mari must have been the person who fetched Peter at the Silent Woman, on whose behalf Jack dropped his by-the-book persona to let Peter off with a warning. A gnawing sense of jealousy began clawing its way through my gut. I know it was mostly my fault, but when Jack and I had hugged just a few minutes before, it was self-conscious and hesitant, but he hugged Mari in front of God and everyone, swinging her up off the floor in his exuberance.

It didn't help that, if you squinted, Marigold Aames looked an awful lot like Rachel, the perky nutritionist my longtime fiancé had run off with.

"Nice to meet you," Rena said, breaking the awkward silence. "And thanks for breaking up whatever was going on over there."

Eyebrows raised, Rena couldn't have been any more transparent in her effort to fish some information from Mari.

"Oh, that," Mari responded with a dismissive wave. "Things are always tense right before a show starts. Now, I hate to be rude, but I have to skedaddle. There's still so much to do before tomorrow morning. But *you*," she said, pointing a waggling finger in Jack's direction, "you have to let me buy you lunch or dinner before I leave town."

Jack shot me a sidelong glance. "Sure. Absolutely."

As Marigold scampered off, my excitement for the cat show diminished considerably. Nothing good could come from this, I thought. Nothing good.

CHAPTER
Two

Knowing how busy I would be for the rest of the week, I decided to have dinner with my sisters, Lucy and Dru, that night. We met at the Koi Pond, a surprisingly authentic Chinese restaurant within walking distance of my house.

When we're together, the McHale sisters are quite a sight, so close in age and appearance, our mother calls us her Irish triplets. We're all tall, but not equally so. Lucy, the baby, is five foot nine, I'm five foot ten, and Dru, the eldest, is five foot eleven. Perfect stair steps, each with long black hair and eyes the color of new spring leaves.

But despite our physical similarities, our temperaments couldn't be further apart. Growing up, we called Dru "Dru the Shrew." She's not really a shrew at all, but she was the tattletale in the family, always strictly abiding by the rules and crying foul when one of us strayed from the straight and narrow. She'd grown into a tense woman, still scrupulously following rules as an accountant and still refusing to sugar-coat anything.

My younger sister, Lucy, earned the moniker "Lucky Lucy." Everything she did ultimately turned in her favor. She never got caught sneaking out to go to post-curfew parties, and she always managed to convince our parents that the degenerate losers she chose to date were, in fact, good and honest boys. As an adult, she'd calmed her wild ways and started dating more respectable boys. Specifically, she'd been dating Xander Stephens—an entrepreneur and all-around good guy. Xander's thin frame towered above Lucy, and he was silent in the face of Lucy's nonstop sarcastic color commentary. They seemed to fit perfectly, her yin to his yang. But, still, Lucy's high spirits were not completely gone: she'd confessed to skinny-dipping in Lake Superior on a recent girls' trip to Duluth, the only one of her circle of friends willing to take the actual plunge.

"How are you holding up?" Dru asked as we slid into the booth. "You're going to be spread pretty thin these next few days."

"I'm okay. Wanda"—our teenaged assistant—"will hold down the store, and Rena's covering the booth at the show. I'm a floater, and I'll be walking around the show passing out cards and making connections."

Lucy laughed. "I never thought I'd see the day when Dizzy Izzy McHale would be the face of a company." Kids at school had started calling me Dizzy Izzy after I spun around too many times on the playground and upchucked on Sean Tucker, but my family had picked up the nickname and used it to tease me about being a little flaky.

"I'm not Dizzy Izzy anymore, Lucy. Now I'm Busy Izzy. Trendy Tails is in the black, even after Rena and I take a small salary for ourselves. We're not rolling in dough, but getting the word out about our store through this cat show will raise our profile considerably."

"I don't know," Dru said, her pessimistic side showing. She set her napkin in her lap and picked up her fork, turning it over and over in her hand the way some people roll coins to soothe themselves. "If you start getting too many orders, how will you fulfill them? You can only sew for so many hours in a day."

I raised my hands in surrender. "Enough. My business is fine, and it's *my* business. You two are just going to have to trust me that I can handle this. Aunt Dolly does."

"For a while Aunt Dolly believed the checkout girl at the Rainbow was an alien," Lucy quipped.

I sighed. "That was only because she heard the girl

speaking Hungarian on the phone, and she realized her mistake almost right away. I know that Aunt Dolly is eccentric and sometimes a bit naive, but she's got a good head on her shoulders. She believed in me enough to invest in the company, and you know how frugal she is."

"Speaking of which," Dru said, "have you paid her back yet?"

"Not that it's any of your business, but we have a repayment plan and I haven't missed a single payment. By this time next year, Dolly will have recovered her investment plus a little extra in lieu of interest."

At that point, our server came to take our orders. I opted for a Szechuan eggplant while both Lucy and Dru ordered the house special: a stir-fried beef dish covered with the most delicious sauce known to man.

"Okay, I don't want to talk about Trendy Tails anymore," Lucy said. "Boring."

"Well, what would you like to discuss, Lucinda?" Dru replied in her most schoolmarmish tone.

"Boys!"

"Ugh." Dru let her fork drop to the table.

"Yes, sister, I want to talk about boys. Like the boy I saw you having coffee with at Joe Time yesterday." My ears perked up. This was news to me.

Dru blushed. "That was Donovan. He works at the credit union. It was just coffee."

"This time," Lucy said. "But what about when Xander saw you with him at Red, White and Bleu?"

If it were possible, Dru's hair would have been blushing by this point. Personally, I was stunned. I couldn't remember the last time my uptight sister had dated.

"Fess up," I said.

Dru closed her eyes and exhaled sharply. "Very well. I guess Merryville's too small to be discreet. Donovan and I have been seeing each other about a month now."

"A month?" Lucy and I cried in unison.

"Yes. Like I said, we were *trying* to be discreet. He's a nice man, goes to church regularly, has a quiet sense of humor . . . and a six-year-old daughter named Naomi."

The server dropped our egg rolls at the table, and we all took a few minutes to enjoy the sweet and salt of the roll and its sauce while we let this bit of information sink in.

"A daughter," I finally said. "That's heavy."

Dru nodded. "I know. At first I thought it would be a deal breaker. But I've met Naomi, and she's just like her dad. Only shorter and with more hair." We all chuckled, breaking the tension. "Seriously, she's a gem. She seems to be okay with me hanging around now and then, and Donovan and I aren't serious yet."

Lucy pounced. "Yet?"

"Yet. And maybe we never will be. But for now I'm enjoying being an honorary member of this little family."

"I think that's great," I said. "For what it's worth, if you do get serious, you'd make a really good mom."

Lucy moaned. "That child will need her aunt Lucy to liven up her life a little. You'll certainly keep her safe and well loved, but a kid's got to have a little adventure in her life."

Dru held up a hand. "No *Aunt Lucy* yet. Like I said, Donovan and I aren't serious yet."

"Yet," Lucy repeated.

Desperate to deflect the attention away from herself, Dru turned to me with wide eyes. "How about you and Jack Collins? Is that serious?"

"I think so," I said, dipping my egg roll in the little ramekin of brilliant ruby-colored sauce.

"You think so?" Lucy held up her hand and started ticking off points on her fingers. "You spend practically every waking minute with the man. He stops by Trendy Tails at least three times a day while he's supposedly keeping Merryville safe. And he's become a regular fixture at Sunday dinners at Mom and Dad's."

"I know. I'm pretty sure it's serious. But just today he agreed to go on a date with another woman."

I felt tears welling in my eyes as our server replaced our appetizer plates with platters of savory beef and eggplant.

"What are you talking about?" Lucy said, her voice as cold and flat as iron. "If he's toying with you, I'll kill him."

Dru leaned forward. "Tell us exactly what happened."

I explained about Marigold Aames being an old college friend of Jack's, about the implication that their relationship had been more than just friendly, and how he'd agreed to go to lunch with her.

Dru and Lucy exchanged a glance and then both threw back their heads and laughed.

"It's not funny."

"Yes, it is," Dru said.

Lucy reached across the table to take my hand. "He didn't say yes to a date. He said yes to lunch. And after she asked him in front of a huge crowd of witnesses, what else could he do? Can you imagine how awkward it would have been if he'd said no? Relax."

Dru nodded. "The moral of this story is that you have strong feelings for Jack Collins. It's making you touchy. Prickly."

"Possessive," Lucy added.

My sisters were right. I was starting to fall hard for Jack Collins.

CHAPTER
Three

I was so excited about the prospect of big sales at the cat show—and, admittedly, a little anxious about this Marigold Aames and what she could mean for my relationship with Jack—that I had a hard time sleeping that night. I finally gave up around five thirty and crawled out of my bed and into the shower. I cringed when the old pipes began singing. I didn't want to wake my downstairs neighbors, Ingrid and Harvey Nyquist.

Ingrid had been my mentor for years, and she owned the building in which I lived and worked. Now in her early eighties, she'd finally gotten around to marrying her high school sweetheart. The two had been separated when Harvey's parents sent him off to military school, and each had lived a full life complete with other spouses. But in their widowhood, the wonders of social media had brought them back together and their teenage love had been rekindled.

While Ingrid and Harvey planned to spend much of the year in Harvey's condo in Boca Raton, they had the apartment on the second floor of 801 Maple in which to spend the dog days of summer. They knew what they were getting into, but I was still self-conscious that they were sandwiched in between the hubbub of the first-floor shop and the noise my animals and I generated in our third-floor apartment. They were retirees, after all.

Because of my early rise, I was ready for the day at an obscenely early hour. I made my way down to the shop and did a little work rearranging my wares on the shelf. I had just settled down with a cup of coffee and the *Merryville Gazette* when there was a sharp knock at the front door.

I looked out, expecting to find Wanda Knight, the Merryville high schooler Rena and I had hired to help out with the business so we would have more time to bake, sew, and market. Wanda would be covering the shop during the cat show, manning the fort while Rena and I were out at the hotel.

Needless to say, I was startled to find Phillip Denford on my front porch. Given his fight with Pris the night before, I was a bit timid about opening the door, but I was relying on this man's cat show to bring in enough working capital to expand my online business presence, allowing people to place orders and make payments directly online without having to call the store.

Xander Stephens owned the Spin Doctor, the record store across the back alley from Trendy Tails. He'd made his store a success by maintaining a thriving online business. He'd offered to do the programming for me, create a shopping cart and secure checkout process, for free, but I couldn't abuse his good nature like that. I knew the offer came at least in part because he was dating my sister Lucy, and it wouldn't be right to take advantage of that situation. I would get him to help me, but only when I could afford to pay him what he was worth.

"Mr. Denford? Please come in."

I held the door and he walked in, hands clasped at the small of his back, scanning the inside of my shop with a proprietary air. King of the hill. Cock of the walk.

His plumage befitted his strut: orange-and-blue plaid pants with a perfectly matched orange golf shirt and blue jacket. Only rich people could get away with that kind of getup. Rich people and my aunt Dolly.

Phillip's perusal of Trendy Tails included a leisurely sweep over my breasts. I suppressed a shudder. I'd met some skeevy guys in my day, but he was just so nonchalant about the way he ogled me, confident that I wouldn't call him out on his bad behavior. As though I might consider it flattering.

"You keep a tidy shop, Ms. McHale. I respect that."

"Thank you?" I was so off-kilter at having Denford in my store—and staring at my bosom—that the words came out as a question.

"I also admire your, ah, product," he continued. He chuckled at his own double entendre. "When Pamela Rawlins returned from her first site visit raving about the cute clothes and accessories you were creating, I purchased a huge selection of your stock."

Phillip Denford had been one of my customers? I racked my brain, trying to remember all my biggest orders, and then it jumped out at me: an online/over-the-phone purchase made late last spring. The caller had ordered one of each of my handmade products—for both dogs and cats—but hadn't purchased any of the items I got from wholesalers. I remembered being flattered that the person liked my work so much. But I also remembered that the caller was a woman. Mari Aames? Most likely.

"Well, thank you for that. I'm honored."

"You should be. I admire your concepts so much that I've sourced them to a manufacturer in Korea."

"What?" It was like his words weren't even in English.

"I've sourced them to a manufacturer so I can produce them and sell them through my own online retail outlets, the Dapper Dog and the Classy Cat." He brought his hands around to the front of his body, revealing the cat pajamas he held. He reached out and pressed the garment into my hand and wrapped my numb fingers around it.

It took only a quick glance for me to recognize the seaming pattern in the pants and the piping detail at the neck, which were a mirror of my own product, but these pajamas were in a flannel pattern I'd never used.

"I don't understand. You're telling me you're going to sell my designs?"

"Well, obviously they won't be exactly your designs. For example, we'll line the Pooch Parkas with synthetic sherpa, not genuine fleece. And you'll note that the pajamas you're holding have a notch at the front of the collar, which your design did not have."

"You can't do this," I said. "It's got to be against the law."

He held up a hand and waggled it back and forth. "Maybe it's on the line, but that line is pretty wobbly, Ms. McHale. Fashion law hasn't really found its stride yet. As I said, we're making some select design changes, and we're not planning to sell the items under the Trendy Tails trademark, so I think we're safe. But even if we're not, even if we are crossing some vague legal line, what exactly do you plan to do about it?"

I shook my head in confusion. "Sue!"

"Mmmm-hmmm. Have you ever been involved in intellectual-property litigation?"

"No."

"Yes, well, it's a lengthy process. You'd need a lawyer. At least one. Preferably a fashion lawyer, and they don't come cheap—and I'm not sure they come in 'Minnesotan' at all. Not to mention the textile, pet, and apparel experts you'd need. From what Pamela said, you're doing good business, but you haven't been open even a full year. There's no way your business has the sort of reserves to fight an IP battle with an established company. Not to mention that my people inform me that you're not independently wealthy. I don't see how you could hold out against someone with my resources."

"You've been looking into my personal finances? How dare you?"

"I assure you all of my inquiries have been legal. For example, a simple title search tells me you don't own this building, that you're renting both your business space and your home. It was also easy enough to find out about the various complaints your neighbor Richard Greene has filed against your business. Complaints that have surely cost you money to resolve."

It was true. Richard Greene owned the Greene Brigade, a shop dedicated to military history and memorabilia. Despite owning a giant German shepherd named MacArthur, Richard was leery of loud and smelly critters possibly running off his clients. He'd tried to oust Trendy Tails from the neighborhood a couple of times. He'd stopped his crusade against us when he decided that it was more fun wooing my aunt Dolly, but his efforts had cost us a pretty penny.

I was still having trouble wrapping my brain around the disaster that was unfolding before me. "But how can you do something like that? Just stealing someone else's hard work. How can you sleep at night?"

"Like a baby, Ms. McHale. A baby who knows that his investment is going to pay off. It's one of the first things you learn in business school: know your competitors."

When I was first opening Trendy Tails, Ingrid told me that the first rule of business was to sell a quality product for a fair price. I liked her school of thought a whole lot better than Denford's.

"If you're dead set on stealing my designs and so certain that you can do so with impunity, why are you bothering to tell me? Is this some sort of negotiation?"

"No negotiation, I'm afraid. Look, I'm not completely heartless—"

"Close enough."

He *tsk*ed at me. "Ms. McHale. I could have done exactly as you suggest and simply allowed you to find out about my business plans through regular channels, but I'm doing you the courtesy of giving you a little warning. You'll probably turn a tidy profit over the course of the M-CFO's convention, and what you *do* with that profit might depend on the future of your business. Do you want to reinvest it in your store and possibly waste it all, or do you want to hold back the profit so you can walk away from your business without going bankrupt?"

I raised my chin a notch, hands balled into fists at my sides. "What makes you think your knockoffs will hurt my business? People recognize quality when they see it."

"They do, indeed. And they'll pay for it, especially if they have money to burn. But I can offer them a product that is almost exactly the same, very high quality, at a fraction of the price, and even rich people like a good deal. For example, that product you are holding? In my online store, it will retail for eighteen dollars."

I studied the pajamas in my hand. He was correct that the quality was high. The seams were reinforced, the piping smooth, the snaps down the back lined up perfectly. If I didn't know better, I would have thought it had come from my own store, from my own hands. The big difference was that I had to sell the pajamas for twenty-five dollars in order to make a profit.

"It's all about mass manufacturing." He pointed to my worktable, where the pattern pieces for my most recent creation were spread out, each piece of paper pinned to the back of a piece of fabric. "Your prices are incredibly high for what amounts to a novelty item, and still, given your in-house manufacturing, I imagine that your profit margins are slim. You can't possibly afford to lower your prices to meet mine. Not without a huge infusion of capital that would allow you to follow my manufacturing strategy."

He smiled. "Even then, if people can buy the same product for the same price at two locations, they're going to use the retailer who is most convenient. My Web sites get massive amounts of traffic, and visitors can purchase both the cute duds *and* all of their grooming supplies, gourmet food, and accessories like crates and bedding. I offer one-stop shopping. You do not."

I may not have had a degree in business, but I wasn't an idiot. Everything Phillip Denford said made intuitive sense. I was turning a profit, but a small one. If he ate into my business even ten percent, it could push me into the red.

Somewhere outside, a car honked, and Phillip leaned back to glance out Trendy Tails' front window.

"That would be for me." He held out his hand for the pajamas, and I dropped them there, careful not to touch him. I was genuinely repulsed by the man.

He paused in the doorway on his way out. "I will see you later at the show, Ms. McHale. For now, consider yourself warned."

CHAPTER
Four

Phillip's visit and the news he brought had thrown me for a vicious loop, a loop that required caffeine to settle, so I'd stopped for a latte on my way to the show. Between that stop and Wanda showing up nearly fifteen minutes after she'd promised to be there, I arrived at the ballroom a few minutes later than expected, fumbling into the room with my arms full. I'd brought Jinx, my black-and-white Norwegian forest cat, to model my wares. She was penned up in a black wire cage to prevent her from slithering off into trouble, but she didn't seem to mind. She groomed herself vigorously, ignoring the people who stopped to admire her fur-trimmed purple track jacket.

"Let's get this party started," Rena said.

I knew I needed to tell Rena about Phillip's threat.

Heck, it wasn't even a threat. . . . It was a plan he'd already put into action, and my business partner had a right to know about it. But the time and place were all wrong. Rena had a good head on her shoulders, but she also had a wicked temper. I was afraid if I told her about Phillip in the midst of the ballroom, she'd storm off to find the man and punch him right in the face. No, it would be better to wait until we were alone and break it to her gently.

"You betcha," I replied, trying to muster some enthusiasm for the day.

Even though the day's events were all agility-based circuits and would be held out in the tent the hotel had set up in its scenic green space, the ballroom buzzed with excitement as breeders and owners took turns making the rounds, checking out the competition, collecting business cards, inquiring about goods and services on display, and, of course, stopping to admire the grand prize for the entire event.

Despite being a total sleazebag, Phillip Denford had outdone himself. He'd had Jolly Nielson, our local jeweler and Rena's girlfriend, create a custom collar dangle. According to Rena, the actual design had been conceived and drawn by Phillip's artist son, Peter. This was no ordinary collar dangle: crafted of the most delicate platinum filigree and set with both a five-carat fancy-cut diamond and a five-carat Colombian emerald, it was a work of art. Very expensive art.

Jolly had even made a platinum cage to house the accessory. Hanging from the top of the cage, the pendant could twist and turn ever so slightly, catching the lights surrounding it from a host of angles. It certainly looked expensive, but its true value wouldn't be known until the end of the show, when it was presented to the grand-prize winner. At that point, a gemologist and an insurance adjuster would swoop in to make the determination of the dangle's cash value and make sure it was insured before the winner even left the room.

The prize had been artfully situated atop a table near the best-in-show ring. The table was draped with pale pink satin gathered in sensuous fabric curls on the table's surface. The cage had been set atop tiered satin-covered boxes, and the whole setting was filled with crystal vases of pink peonies, white lilies, and delicate green Kermit mums. The arrangement looked like something out of a fairy tale, and it seemed out of place surrounded by the chaos of the show.

The only thing marring the tablescape was a paper cup from Joe Time Coffee that someone had carelessly left on the corner. I walked over and snatched up the cup, still half-full of milky coffee, and walked it to the large waste can just behind our station. I thought about tucking it behind Jinx's cage in case someone came back for it, but frankly, it smelled funky, like someone had dripped perfume into it. It reminded me of my friend Taffy's Happy Leaf Tea Shoppe, a faintly musty and cloying smell. Near as I could tell, the stuff had gone off and should probably be tossed, and if someone still thought it was any good and came back to claim it, I would take the heat.

"Thanks! I was just about to do the same thing so I could get a clean picture."

I looked up to find Ama Olmstead, a reporter for the *Merryville Gazette*, facing the prize table with her sleek digital camera in hand. The petite Danish woman, pixie cute, used to carry a slew of camera equipment with her back when her strapping husband, Steve Olmstead, had been available to help her lug it around. Steve and Ama were divorced now, though, and the single mom had had to pare down her life in a multitude of ways, from moving into a smaller house to limiting herself to one really good camera for her assignments.

"How have you been, Ama?"

"As well as can be expected," she said with a half smile. "I've been meaning to tell you that Jordan has started calling Packer 'his' dog." We both laughed. Ama's toddler son often played with Packer when the pooch and I ran into the Olmsteads in Dakota Park. Packer was great with children, and Ama had often expressed gratitude that Jordan would grow up loving dogs instead of fearing them.

"Are you thinking about getting him his own?"

"Someday. When he's old enough to walk it and scoop its poop. Right now I have my hands full, and I'm happy for him to simply have the occasional play-date with Packer."

"Well, anytime you want some canine companionship, you know my number. Packer has boundless energy, so he's always game for a romp in the park."

"Thanks for that." She swept her hand in an all-encompassing gesture. "This is quite the show, isn't it?"

"I had no idea," I confided. "I figured it would be big and good for business, but I had no idea just how big it would be."

She grinned at me. "Want a little free promo? I can get a picture of you and Rena at your booth."

"Oh my gosh! Would you?"

One of the lessons I had learned during my months as an entrepreneur was that one never turned down the chance for free publicity.

"Rena," I called. "Ama wants to get a shot of us in front of our booth."

"Ooh! Fun!" Rena replied, scrambling around from the back of the table. "Here—let me get your bangs straightened." To my horror, she licked a finger and used it to sweep a swath of hair from my face.

"Rena!"

"Oh, chill out," she muttered.

Ama was laughing so hard she was bent at the

waist and wiping her eyes. "You two should take this show on the road," she said when she came up for air.

I held up a kitty capelet while Rena pretended to take a bite out of a salmon cracker, and Ama snapped our picture.

"I need to scoot off to take some pictures of the cats and guests. But it was great seeing the two of you."

"Same here, Ama."

"Where's Pris?" I asked Rena as Ama made her way out through the crowd. I could see all her worker bees buzzing around the spa station in the corner of the ballroom, but I couldn't spot Pris in the midst of the fray. I felt a stab of irritation. We'd made an arrangement to share each other's cards with the cat owners, and if someone bought a service from Pris and an item from me, they got ten percent off both purchases. I had my cards ready to go, but Pris still hadn't brought hers over.

"I don't know," Rena replied. "I saw her when I first got here this morning, but it's such a zoo in here I can barely keep track of myself."

Tension in the ballroom continued to mount as we all waited for an announcement that the day's activities were beginning. But I didn't see anyone in charge. I expected to see Pamela Rawlins, her brown Burmese, Tonga, draped around her neck. She was technically the organizer of the event. I scanned the room, looking for signs of her sin-black topknot moving through the crowd, but nothing.

Neither Marsha nor Phillip Denford had made an appearance yet, and Marigold Aames—who seemed to be the driving force of the Denford operation—was MIA, too. The only Denford in sight was Peter, and he stood off to the side, in an empty judging circle, sipping a cup of coffee.

I frowned. My sixth sense told me something was up.

I reached beneath our table to grab a box of outfits, thinking I might find a wardrobe change for Jinx for later in the day. As I picked it up, I thought I heard a rustling sound coming from inside. I set the box on the table and cautiously lifted a corner open. In a wink, something small and furry wiggled out from the confines of the box and leapt from the edge of the table.

My first thought was that Rena's ferret, Val, had hitchhiked to the show in the box, but then I realized that Rena would have left Val at home for the day and that the critter who'd scampered from the box was too small to be a ferret.

"Was that Gandhi?" Rena squealed.

Lord have mercy. It absolutely was Gandhi, making one of his rare and inopportune appearances.

Nearly a year before, a woman named Sherry Harper

had died in my back alley, and her auburn guinea pig, Gandhi, had escaped into the wild. Over the months, we'd tried to catch him as he took up residence in businesses up and down the alley: Richard Greene's Greene Brigade, then my friend Taffy's tea shop, and eventually in Xander Stephens's record shop, Spin Doctor. I lived in fear that he'd find his way to Ken West's restaurant, Red, White & Bleu, and end up in an exterminator's crosshairs.

I hadn't seen Gandhi inside Trendy Tails since he first went missing, but somehow he must have gotten in and managed to elude Jinx for long enough to hop a ride to the M-CFO cat show.

The absolute last place a guinea pig should be.

I crouched down to see if I could spot the little fella, but between the table drapes and the sea of legs, he was long gone.

"Lose something?" I looked up to find Jack smiling down at me.

"Yes. No. Sort of," I muttered as I climbed to my feet. Jack stood next to my aunt Dolly, who—alarmingly—held Packer, my pug-bulldog mix, on a leash.

I hugged everyone in sight, including my dog, who returned my affection with a big slobbery puppy kiss, before narrowing my eyes and chiding Jack and Dolly. "Why did you bring Packer?"

Jack shoved his hands in the pockets of his cargo

shorts and shrugged. "Don't look at me. I'm just the driver."

Right. "Just the driver." Like he had no control over Dolly, no obligation to rein her in. Jack knew Dolly did inappropriate things on a daily basis; it took a village to keep Dolly in check. Besides, Jack was a cop, for heaven's sake. He should have been the voice of reason. But I was inclined to give him a pass. Once Dolly got an idea in her head, it was hard to talk her out of it. In fact, the more rational you tried to be, the more she dug in her heels. While Jack was very serious about his copness, he wasn't a bully; I couldn't imagine him forcing Dolly to do something she didn't want to do.

For her part, Dolly cocked her white-haired head and narrowed her eyes right back at me. "Izzy McHale. I never knew you to be so discriminatory. Packer has just as much right to be here as anyone else."

"But it's a cat show." I knew I was stating the obvious, but what else could I say? I swept my arm around to display the tables full of cats.

"And I'm sure all the cats are lovely," Dolly said. "But Packer wanted to join in on the fun, and you know he'll be a perfect gentleman."

I knew nothing of the sort. Both Packer and Jinx were ill-behaved little creatures, spoiled rotten by Ingrid, Dolly, and occasionally me. Besides, even assuming we could corral Packer under our display table, I knew his presence would disturb the cats.

Sure enough, Packer let out a snuffling little bark, and the cats in the cages closest to my table started to *roo*. The international feline call of distress spread from cage to cage, table to table, until the collective keening of two hundred cats overwhelmed the room. Even Jinx had her ears flattened back on her skull, and she usually ignored Packer like he was a piece of furniture.

As though the cat calls had summoned her, Pamela Rawlins strode into the ballroom through the main door, about twenty feet from my table. She had her eyes downcast and her shoulders hunched with tension as she made a beeline toward the prize table. She leaned in to examine the glittering collar dangle, head cocked this way and then that, before turning on her heel and walking back the way she'd come.

I heard sniggering behind me and turned to find both Rena and Jack, heads down, shoulders shaking suspiciously. "You two are not helping," I hissed. "Dolly, you have got to take Packer home."

"But I want to stay."

I pinned Jack with a stern look. "Jack will take you back to 801 Maple so you can drop off Packer and leave him with Wanda, and then he will bring you back to the show. Right?"

"Yes, ma'am," he said, scuffing his toe like a wayward child.

Before they could move, a *thunk*ing sound resonated from the hallway, and the lights in the ballroom went out. In the vast windowless room, there wasn't so much as a glimmer of light. After a heartbeat of silence, both the cats *and* the people began to whine and call out, everyone disoriented in the sudden darkness. Not to be outdone, Packer took up a howling complaint.

I felt a rush of air as someone moved quickly past me. I was disoriented by the dark, but I got the distinct impression that the person was moving from my right—from somewhere near the main ballroom door—to my left—toward the back corner of the ballroom, where the conformation-judging rings started to wend their way around the room, forming a big U that ended right by the other front corner of the room, where Pris's grooming station had been arranged.

A minute later, I was blinded by light from the corridor as Jack threw open the main doors and secured them to the heavy magnets set in the wall. A maintenance worker rushed up to him, and the two exchanged a few brief words.

Slowly that beacon of light from the doorway lowered the level of chaos in the room. Jack yelled out across the crowd, "Just a tripped fuse, everyone." Everyone hushed, and it seemed like all attention—human and feline—had turned to Jack. I felt a swell of pride at his confidence, the way he commanded the room. "We'll have light again in a second."

As his last syllable trailed away, there was another *thunk*, and the lights returned, leaving a roomful of people blinking as their eyes readjusted to the bright ballroom chandeliers.

"On that note," Jack said, "we'd better get going. Heaven forbid the lights go off again and we lose Packer in the ensuing panic." He gently took Dolly's elbow and, like the big Boy Scout he was, drew her toward the wide-open entrance to the ballroom.

Dolly and Jack were almost to the door when Packer suddenly let out a yip and pulled away from Dolly, ripping his leash from her hands. Dolly looked back at me in helpless horror as Packer did a joyous pirouette and landed in a crouch, ready to sprint off to heaven knows where.

Great. I get invited to a potentially life-altering cat show, and I manage to release both a guinea pig and a dog into the mix within the first hour. Brilliant. At least the lights were on.

Without hesitation, I dashed after the dog, praying I'd get to him before he knocked over a table and sent a dozen cats hurtling through space. He started to scamper behind the table holding the grand-prize collar dangle, so I made an end run around the other side, trying to cut him off.

When I reached the back of the table, only a few feet from the ballroom wall, I realized Packer wasn't running anymore. He'd found what he was looking for.

Packer sat, restlessly shifting his little body from haunch to haunch and occasionally licking his chops with his long taffylike tongue. Right at his feet, a plaid pant leg protruded from underneath the table.

My heart caught in my throat. I reached out a toe to nudge the leg, but I got no response. Passed out, or dead? There was only one way to know.

I stood on my tiptoes, caught Jack's eye, and beckoned him over. A mischievous smile played across his lips and he gave me a suggestive wink as he walked across the room to join me, but when I pointed at the leg, he sobered right up. Dashing Jack disappeared and Detective Collins took charge.

He met my eyes and, without either of us saying a word, we bent down. That's when I saw the rusty brown flecks that stained the blush-colored satin puddling on the floor. Jack lifted the fabric with two fingers, and we both peered under the table.

There lay Phillip Denford in a viscous pool of blood, a scrap of white cloth clutched in his hand and what appeared to be a pair of grooming sheers sticking straight out of his neck. I knew dead when I saw it, and Phillip was deader than disco.

I suddenly felt woozy. Alas, this was not the first time I'd been so close to a dead body, but it was the first time I'd been so close to so much blood, and the scent rested like a bad penny on my tongue. A mixture of horror and fear seared my blood. I stood up, maybe a bit too quickly, and caught my balance on the edge of the table. The stand holding the grand prize teetered precariously from my jostling, and I snatched out a hand to hold it steady.

And that's when I saw that the jeweled collar dangle was gone.

CHAPTER
Five

For the first three hours, the ballroom was a madhouse. The Merryville PD had set up a flimsy perimeter of crime-scene tape to cordon off the front corner of the room, where we'd found Phillip Denford and lost the hundred-thousand-dollar collar dangle. I don't know what I was expecting them to use, but I'd gotten the same yellow plastic tape at Parties Plus for Aunt Dolly's most recent birthday party. It made the cops' stuff seem oddly unofficial.

That impression was heightened by the low police presence. A group of officers was out on Highway 59 working a multicar-semitruck accident that had traffic backed up for miles in either direction, and another group had gone down to the Twin Cities to get trained in using the new body cams the department had purchased. Jack was the only detective on-site, and he was dressed so casually, in cargo shorts and a pale green Henley, that he didn't look like any kind of cop at all. I counted a meager three officers and two crime-scene techs, including the poor officer trying to man the door to the ballroom.

As soon as the first uniformed officer had shown up, cell phones had emerged from pockets and purses in a wave. Everyone involved with the cat show—from trainers to owners to random family members—knew that something big was happening in the ballroom, and everyone wanted to join the crowd inside so they could watch the drama unfold. The problem was there were two doors off the main hotel hallway that led into the ballroom: the main door up by my vendor table, which opened directly into the crime scene, and the one at the far end of the ballroom, which opened into the space in which Pris had set up her grooming operation. Two doors and only one officer, who was splitting his attention between guarding the main doorway and watching what was taking place behind the prize table.

In short, a steady flow of gawkers had made their way past Prissy's Pretty Pets, swelling the crowd to nearly twice the size it had been when the first hue and cry had been raised.

Dolly didn't want to miss a single detail, so she managed to worm her way to the front of the crowd, closest to Phillip's body. "It's research," she said. "Research for when I become a PI." Personally, I'd been present at enough crime scenes that the actual mechanics didn't particularly interest me. In fact, they nauseated me. I put Rena in charge of Dolly, making sure Dolly didn't plunge past the crime-scene tape to "help," while I fell to the back of the crowd, tugging Packer along behind me.

When I got clear of the horde, I knelt down to give Packer some loving. He waggled his little butt while I scratched his ears and cooed praises for being such an observant dog. He'd rolled over on his back for a good belly rub when I heard the weeping.

I turned to find Marsha Denford, Pamela Rawlins, and Mari Aames, all of whom must have found their way into the ballroom after Phillip's body had been found. They stood in the same general area, but they didn't seem to be together: no hugs, no clasped hands, not even any eye contact. Tears poured from Mari's red-rimmed eyes, her cheeks mottled and the knot of honey hair on top of her head askew. Pamela's thin crimson lips pressed into a straight, harsh line. She shifted from foot to foot while her fingers flew over the screen of her smartphone. Both were obviously upset.

Marsha's behavior was the exact opposite. She also shifted her weight from foot to foot, but it appeared she was simply swaying softly. Her eyes were flat and glazed, and she was making strange pouty expressions with her mouth, twisting her lips this way and that. I couldn't imagine what it was like to lose the man you loved, so I hated to judge, but I'd been to college and I knew what "high" looked like.

I stood and walked Packer toward them. He seemed to pick up the mood and became uncharacteristically calm. He homed in on Mari, the one in the most apparent distress, and dropped to his haunches at her feet. She knelt down to greet him, burying her face in his bristly fur, and began to keen softly. "I don't even like dogs," she muttered as she clutched my boy close.

"How are you two doing?" I asked Marsha and Pamela.

Pamela scowled briefly at me before turning her attention back to her phone, her fingers never pausing. Even in the broiling summer heat, she was dressed in unrelieved black, a single pendant—what appeared to be a gold locket, a cat etched on its face—her only nod to femininity.

Marsha offered a bleary smile. "You're so kind to ask." A pale breath of laughter escaped her. "No one else has bothered."

That struck me as hard to believe, but Marsha did have a standoffish nature. And, frankly, she didn't seem particularly upset (though I suspect that had more to do with whatever had shrunken her pupils to pinpricks than with her actual emotional state).

"I think I'm fine," she continued. "There's so little point in being anything else."

I didn't expect such a Zen-like response from Phillip Denford's pampered wife. She looked every inch the socialite. Her long red hair had been pulled back in a classic French twist; her vibrant red, low-heeled sandals and matching mani-pedi added a playful touch to her cream-and-navy linen dress; and pearls the size of Concord grapes hugged her earlobes. The only thing marring her look was what appeared to be a small hole by the right shoulder of her dress. What's more, close-up I could see that her eyes tilted up ever so slightly and the skin on her cheekbones was pulled tight as a drum. Marsha couldn't have been more than forty, but she'd already had her first face-lift.

"Can I get you anything? Some water or a chair? I'd offer to help you get closer to the investigation, but I'm not sure that's anything you'd want to see."

My words elicited another muffled wail from Mari.

"I'm just fine, dear. I don't think we've had the pleasure."

Over the four months of planning the cat show, we'd met at least a half-dozen times.

"My name is Izzy McHale. I own Trendy Tails, the pet boutique here in town."

"Oh, of course. Where is my head? Izzy. Phillip spoke highly of you."

Given my brief interactions with Phillip, he might have spoken highly of my breasts—which he had studied like an appraiser might study a piece of sculpture he was valuing—but he certainly hadn't spoken highly of my brain. Every suggestion either Pris or I made about the show, from layout to schedule to catering, had been quickly dismissed, and he had clearly thought he could run roughshod over me in a bid to steal my business.

Speak of the devil and she shall appear. As if my thoughts had summoned her, Pris sidled up. She was a pale woman, her eggshell skin and platinum hair a perfect foil for her Nordic eyes, but at that moment her face was so bloodless it was almost gray. Her right hand clasped the handles of the leather tote she wore over her left shoulder like she was ready to make a run for it. I even thought I detected a faint tremor in her left hand when she raised it to brush an errant hair from her eyes.

She was still Pris, though, and she looked as polished as new silver in her summer-weight linen pants and blush-colored sleeveless silk blouse, not a drop of sweat showing despite the eighty-five-degree heat outside and her apparent agitation. In her three-inch heels she was able to catch my eye without tilting her head.

"What a mess," she muttered. "I blame you, Izzy."

"Me?" I had found the body, but I didn't see how

that made it my fault. Besides, I was keeping hush about finding Phillip. I didn't want to be mobbed with questions.

"It's your terrible, rotten luck. Everything you touch turns to murder."

"Murder?" Pamela said, her fingers finally going still. "Who said anything about murder? Was Phillip murdered?" she asked, turning to face me head-on.

Everyone in the room knew that Phillip had been found dead behind the prize table, but Jack had sworn me to secrecy regarding the cause of death.

I raised my hands to indicate I had no idea.

"Phillip had a bad heart," Marsha said softly.

"I'm sure his heart was rotten to the core. But with this one"—Pris waved her hand in my direction—"hanging about, it's almost assuredly murder."

Mari finally stood up, her tear-streaked face the very picture of grief. "He can't have been murdered," she whispered. "Everyone admired him."

Even drugged-out Marsha looked at Mari like the girl was crazy. "Admired and liked are not the same thing, Mari. Phillip was a hard man. I'm sure he had enemies. But," she added, raising a hand to forestall any comment Mari might make, "he also had a bad heart. I think we should wait for the police to tell us what's what."

"Well," Pamela said, "whatever killed him, we have

to decide what to do about the show. If it were just a single-day event, we'd obviously cancel."

It seemed obvious to me that the M-CFO would cancel the show no matter how long the event was scheduled to run. You didn't just pick up and carry on after something like this.

"But we've got hundreds of contestants in both the agility competition and the more traditional portion of the show. People have booked out every hotel in Merryville for the next four nights. I've been in touch with everyone else on the board and they agree: we need to proceed."

Marsha, Mari, and Pris all nodded. Apparently, I was the only one who thought the death of the director warranted canceling the event. Before I could voice my suggestion that the whole shindig be canceled, Peter Denford made his way toward our little group. He was walking over from the empty judging ring I'd seen him in earlier, coffee still in tow.

Once again, he was dressed casually in linen and denim. He looked morose, his brooding scowl apparently his default expression, but far from heartbroken. In fact, he lifted the cup of coffee that seemed permanently attached to the end of his arm and took a long swallow before giving us a little wave.

Mari turned and threw herself into his arms. "Oh, Peter. It's horrible. Just horrible. I am so, so sorry for your loss," she wailed, her composure crumbling again.

Peter stood there, towering over Mari, one hand hanging loose at his side, the other held carefully away from his white linen shirt to prevent a fashion disaster from a coffee spill. He looked to his step-mother for guidance, but she just shrugged and offered him a tiny smile.

"Good heavens, Mari," Pamela snapped. "Get yourself together. You're making a scene."

"Please give her some slack, Pamela," Marsha said. "She hasn't been feeling well. She even called this morning to say she'd be late because of a bad stomach, and you know Mari is not one to shirk from work. I think we can all stand to show her some compassion."

Compassionate or not, Peter was not willing to be the shoulder Mari cried upon. Peter wrested himself away from her, managing to extricate himself from the tangle of her arms without spilling a drop. When he was free, he handed her his coffee and pulled his stepmother into a warm embrace. "I'm sorry, Marsha. You know I am."

"I know, darling. Some things just can't be helped."

The two of them turned away from us for a moment, heads bent close in conversation. Peter clasped Marsha's hands, holding them so tightly that I could see the white outline of his knuckles from several feet away.

When he stepped away, Marsha pivoted and collapsed on Pris's shoulder. Pris hesitated a moment, a look of uncertainty on her face, then gently raised her hands to pat Marsha on the back. Marsha clasped Pris to her for several minutes, and all I could think about was how Pris would react to having Marsha's dark eye makeup smeared all over her blush-colored silk shell.

Indeed, when Marsha lifted her head, I caught Pris glancing down at her shoulder, which remained mercifully clean. She caught my eyes as she looked back up, and we exchanged a small knowing smile. We might not be the best of friends, but we'd come to know each other thoroughly since we'd become something like competitors in the Merryville pet-care world.

"Heavens," Pamela said. "Suddenly everyone's best buddies." She sighed before continuing. "Today's a wash, so we'll have to move agility to tomorrow morning. We wanted to have the judging in all the rings spread out so visitors could watch everything, but we'll simply have to double up here and there to make up for lost time. The closing masquerade ball will be held right on schedule."

Holy cats, I thought. *Body or no body, the show must go on.*

Jack stood in the middle of a wide ring of Midwest Cat Fanciers, as though a force field were keeping the milling crowd at bay. By the time Phillip Denford's body had been removed by emergency personnel, everyone involved in the show had heard the news and gathered in the big ballroom despite police efforts to cordon off the scene. Even after a second officer had been dedicated to crime-scene security, guarding the door in Pris's corner of the room, there were just too many back hallways and service entrances to keep would-be rubberneckers out. Still, the burgeoning crowd didn't press in on Jack. The cat-show attendees all wanted to be close enough to him to get the scoop on what was happening, but there was some sort of invisible barrier they didn't want to cross. As though death were catching.

As a result, Jack turned in awkward circles, voice raised, trying to calm everyone down while a couple of county crime-scene techs kept people from backing into the actual taped-off crime scene.

"Did Phillip die during the blackout?" someone asked.

"I really can't comment on the time of death."

I understood where Jack was coming from, but I was pretty sure Phillip's body had been under the table long before the blackout. The blood beneath his body had been dark and sticky-looking, and he wasn't actually bleeding when I saw him.

"But if it was during the blackout, someone should sue the hotel."

"That's really not a question for the police. And it's certainly not something that needs to be resolved right now."

"Was Phillip murdered?" This question came from

the opposite side of the circle as the first, and Jack spun around quickly. I don't know if he was just responding to the question or if he was trying to see which of the dozens of middle-aged women in cat-themed sweatshirts had done the asking.

"Well, it . . ." He trailed off and ran his fingers through his short blond hair. "As I said," he continued, "it would be premature to speculate about the cause and manner of death."

"He had scissors in his neck," said a diminutive woman with hair the color of dryer lint and a pair of gold wire-rimmed glasses. She stood in the front row of the circle and met Jack's gaze dead-on while everyone around her gasped in horror.

"No comment," Jack replied.

That triggered a flurry of smothered cries and whispers. *Scissors, murder, dead,* the crowd breathed. Poor Jack had completely lost control of the situation.

"Can we leave?" someone from the back of the crowd chimed in.

Jack's jaw muscles bunched. "Half of you just showed up, and now you want to leave?" he snapped. He took a deep breath, blowing it out slowly. "I apologize. But the answer is no, you cannot leave. Not until the police have gotten statements from each of you."

"But if there's a murderer in the room, are we even safe?"

"Yes." Jack sighed. "The lights are on and the police are here. You should all be perfectly safe."

Pris Olson stepped inside the fairy ring of onlookers, her beauty-queen features pulled tight in an expression of righteous indignation. "This is ridiculous. You know who we are and where you can find us. Why do we have to wait until everyone has been questioned?"

Jack had little patience for Pris's overblown sense of self-importance. He was a simple man and got a little prickly when others put on airs. "Mrs. Olson," he responded formally, "I am not going to stand here and debate with you about police procedure during an official investigation. But you were planning to spend the day in this room anyway, right?"

"Working," Pris sniped. "I was planning to be here running my booth and earning a living. With the show on hold, we're all just going to be twiddling our thumbs."

"I've got a cribbage board," the bespectacled woman offered helpfully.

Pris's eyelids fluttered. "How nice for you. But I honestly have better . . ." She trailed off, apparently realizing she was about to insult the company of the very cat enthusiasts whose business she wanted to attract.

She sighed. "Lovely. I haven't played cribbage in years." She offered a thin-lipped smile and began taking a step backward into the crowd. As she did so, however, she caught her spiked heel on one of the metal electrical casings that crisscrossed the ballroom floor. For a moment her arms pinwheeled and she tottered first to the left, then to the right. In the end, though, she couldn't save herself: Pris Olson, once the queen bee of all of Merryville, Minnesota, fell flat on her face in front of an entire roomful of cat lovers.

The crowd gasped, one giant collective inhalation. As her knees hit the ground, she reached out her arms to break her fall and, in doing so, lost control over her spacious Coach shoulder bag. The purse slid down her arm, spilling its contents as it, too, struck the ground. Papers and lipstick tubes and even a compact hair iron skittered across the floor. And then . . .

As we all watched in wonder, a shiny silver ball emerged from the recesses of the Coach bag and rolled—wobbling on the delicate wires that composed its surface—straight toward Jack Collins, stopping when it hit his foot.

As one, the crowd exhaled a mighty "oooohhh" and then grew deathly silent.

It was the platinum collar dangle, its diamond and emerald glittering in the bright overhead light, making soft tinkling noises as the dangle got knocked around inside its wire cage and eventually came loose of its mooring to the cage. It was the platinum collar dangle that had gone missing during the blackout, and it had been in Pris Olson's purse.

CHAPTER
Six

"**O**ver my dead body." Jack shifted in his chair, began tipping it back onto its two back legs, but then caught my mother's eye and let the chair fall on all fours.

"Nice turn of phrase," Rena quipped.

Rena, Dolly, Jack, and I were clustered around the table that dominated the Trendy Tails barkery, a space that had once been a dining room, back when the grand old Victorian at 801 Maple had been a single-family residence. The table—a simple pine table painted a glossy cherry red and decorated with hand-painted birds and flowers—had been in this room for as long as I could remember. When Ingrid Whitfield had run the Merryville Gift Haus out of the space, the table had held mountains of hand-knit sweaters, scarves, and mittens. Now it served many purposes: I used it when I was cutting patterns for my hand-tailored pet apparel, Rena occasionally used it to display her homemade organic pet treats, but it was primarily used as a gathering spot for friends and family when the doors to Trendy Tails were locked to the public.

That evening, the four of us sat at the table discussing the day's events while my mother dished out servings of her famous creamy mushroom hotdish. Basically, it was mushroom stroganoff: earthy mushrooms and egg noodles in a hearty herbed cream sauce. My mother, however, would have protested slapping such a highfalutin name on her homespun casserole. She took pride in creating simple home-style fare, and she would assume she was being accused of putting on airs if you'd called her hotdish something so fancy. And, to be fair, Mom parted ways with a traditional stroganoff by making the dish vegetarian, adding green peas and carrots for color, and smothering the top with buttered bread crumbs. I was happy to let her call it whatever she wanted to, because it was one of my favorites, and I didn't want anything to slow the frequency with which she made it. Sticklers might argue that it wasn't a proper dish for a summer supper, but the gusto with which we were all scooping dinner onto our plates made it clear there were no sticklers at the table.

"I'm not kidding, Izzy," Jack said. "You're staying out of this."

I sighed and gave Jinx a gentle nudge to encourage her to jump off my lap. I didn't mind the animals being in the room while we ate, but I didn't want to drip hot mushroom sauce on my cat. "I don't know why you're in such a state, Jack. I'm not about to put on a deerstalker and go looking for clues with a magnifying glass. But I can find out stuff you can't. People clam up when you're around, but it seems they'll say just about anything in front of me. I promise I'm just going to keep my ear to the ground."

Jack glowered at me. Given my past behavior, my promise may have lacked credibility.

"It can't hurt," Dolly added as she ground a generous amount of black pepper over her hotdish. "Jack, you have to admit that we have a pretty good track record in the field of criminal investigation."

Rena snorted and I winced. It had to chafe just a bit that a gang of amateurs had beaten the police at their own game, not once but twice in the past year. Jack never mentioned our sleuthing in those terms, but I'd heard others make cracks about Merryville's new homemaker homicide division.

"You've gotten lucky," Jack said.

"Hey!" Rena, Dolly, and I protested in unison.

The look on Jack's face, the look of a man who's

just realized he's the only man in a roomful of women, would have been comical if he hadn't just dismissed the hard work I'd put into solving those crimes. He looked to the floor where Packer sat wiggling in anticipation of a savory morsel falling to the floor, apparently seeking some sort of solidarity. "I mean," Jack backpedaled, "that you've gotten lucky that you haven't been hurt. Besides, I understand why you were so motivated to snoop in Merryville's last two murders, given Rena and Dolly's involvement"—my friends and family had a terrible knack for looking like killers—"but Pris is hardly part of your inner circle."

"The man has a point," Rena said. "Pass the pepper, please."

Echoes of Phillip Denford's early-morning threats filled my ears. I didn't realize I'd stopped breathing until my lizard brain took over, and I sucked in a gasp of air. Jack was wrong about my desire to get involved in this investigation. It wasn't just about protecting Pris. I had a powerful reason for wanting to hunt for evidence of the real killer—whether that person turned out to be Pris or someone else—but I wasn't prepared to share that reason with my cop boyfriend just yet.

It felt like a betrayal. If we had a solid relationship, it had to be built on trust. I should *trust* Jack with the information I had about Denford's unethical practices; it might actually help with his investigation. But it would also point a blazing orange arrow at my head, identifying me as a possible suspect. One of the very reasons I admired Jack so much was his sense of honesty and integrity. He would have to take the information to the rest of the police department. He might even have to recuse himself from the investigation. Trusting Jack with my story meant trusting the entire Merryville Police Department with my story, and they weren't all dating me.

"I know there's little love lost between me and Pris. That's why I promise I won't get us involved in any crazy shenanigans. Just a little active listening."

My mother set her own plate on the table and plopped down in her chair. "I don't see what good it can do. Poor Pris looks guilty as sin, and if you go poking around, you're just going to antagonize these cat people whom you want to woo. You can't help Pris, but you can sure do some damage to your business prospects."

"Thank you, Mrs. McHale," Jack said with a self-satisfied smile.

"Not so fast, young man," she scolded, one finger raised in a motherly assertion of power. Her tone made Packer whine. "I appreciate you caring about my daughter and trying to keep her safe, but don't go thinking you can tell her what to do. My Izzy has a mind of her own, and she can make her own decisions. And her own mistakes," she added pointedly, staring at the sauce-covered noodle I was casually lowering for Packer. I was a wildly indulgent pet parent, and both Packer and Jinx had the poor manners to prove it.

"Mother!" I hissed.

"Well, it's true. I don't care that your sisters and all your school friends called you Dizzy Izzy," she said, managing to brighten my blush even more. "You're a smart girl and always have been. Just look at what you've done with this business. We all thought you were crazy."

"Mother!"

"Izzy. Clothes for cats?"

"And dogs," Rena added helpfully.

"Right," my mom continued. "You have to admit it sounds like a crazy business, especially for a normal little town like Merryville, but you've actually managed to make it work. We all doubted you—me, your dad, and your sisters—everyone except Aunt Dolly, and look at how wrong we were. I just won't stand for anyone else giving you short shrift."

"I . . . I just—"

Jack raised a hand to halt my flustered response. "Mrs. McHale, I promise you that I would never underestimate Izzy's intelligence. I just worry about the size of her heart. The softy who gives illicit noodles to her dog is the softy who may inadvertently run up against some very bad guys . . . and not realize they're bad guys until it's too late. I want to protect her from that."

"Enough of the smushy-mushy stuff," Rena said. "I just don't think Pris did it."

We all stopped midchew and turned to face her. Rena seemed like the last person on earth to champion Pris's cause.

"What?" Rena said, a forkful of hotdish hovering near her mouth. "Look, Pris is a witch with a capital B and she has fallen on hard times, but what good is stealing a fancy cat ornament going to do her? Where's she going to sell something like that without people asking questions?"

Jack raised his eyebrows. "You seem to have given this a lot of thought."

Rena grinned. "Like Dolly said, we've got some mad investigative skills at this table." She reached out to exchange a fist bump with Dolly, who was cackling like a guinea fowl. "And thanks to my dad's love affair with the bottle, I've met some pretty sketchy people in my time."

"What about poor Mr. Denford's death?" my mom asked. I'd filled her in on the big fight between Denford and Pris the night before. "Stealing the collar ornament may have been out of Pris's comfort zone, but it sounds like she had a real bone to pick with Denford. Between needing money and her public display of animosity toward Phillip Denford, she seems like a prime suspect."

"The murder means Pris definitely isn't the bad guy," Rena said. "Pris never would have killed Denford that way."

"I don't know," Dolly responded. "That Pris Olson is a tough cookie. I can see her whacking someone without batting an eye."

My practical mother gave her fanciful sister a gentle nudge on the arm. "Dorothy. Whacking? You need to stop it with the true-crime television shows." She frowned. "But you make a good point about Pris having enough mean in her to kill someone."

"True," Rena said. "I didn't mean that Pris was above committing murder, but not in the way someone killed Phillip. I don't see scissors as Pris's weapon of choice. Too up close. Too bloody. Pris would pick poison. Or shoot someone from far away. Maybe even conk someone over the head with a heavy object. But she wouldn't get her hands all bloody by stabbing someone."

Jack shook his head. "This is all very clever, Rena. But I've been doing this for ten years now, and if there's one thing I've learned, it's this: when a person is desperate enough, they can do just about anything."

Rena, Jack, Dolly, and my mom all headed for their respective homes. With the doors locked and the dishes done, I pulled out my trusty Singer and sat back at the red table for a sewing session. My mind buzzed with thoughts about Pris, Phillip Denford, and all the horrible things I'd seen that day, and sewing always calmed me.

The talk that evening had inspired me to craft a deerstalker hat for dogs, one that would keep the whole head warm while still allowing for ear mobility. Scraps of corduroy and a sherpa fleece I'd used for snug coats the winter before quickly took shape. I had just run the last seam on my prototype and was debating whether to raid the freezer for a pint of cherry chip or go straight to bed when I heard quiet rapping on the glass portion of the front door.

I looked up, and the warm glow of the porch light revealed Sean Tucker.

I quickly backstitched three or four stitches to hold my seam, snipped the thread that tethered the hat to the machine, and—as I shuffled to the door—plopped the hat on a dog-shaped mannequin perched on a shelf near the front of the store.

"Sean! What brings you out so late at night? Do you want some ice cream?"

"Is that a trick question?" Sean's face lit up with his lopsided grin as he stepped into the store. "I always want ice cream."

It was true. Sean Tucker'd had a raging sweet tooth since I'd first met him in the third grade. I always gave him the trick-or-treat candy that no one in the family wanted—the Mary Janes, the Laffy Taffies, and the Bit-O-Honeys. The remarkable thing is that he could hoover up all that sugar and remain whippet thin. Even now, he was in his early thirties, and his waistline hadn't caught up with his candy addiction.

He followed me into the first-floor kitchen. As I scooped us dishes of ice cream, I studied him out of the corner of my eye. Sean, Rena, and I had been best friends in both middle and high school, our tight bond broken only when Sean decided to declare his love for me and woo me away from my high school sweetheart, Casey Alter. In retrospect, I realized that he'd been right that stormy night, but at the time I was fixated on the happily-ever-after that Casey and I had planned. The event drove a wedge between us that wasn't removed until nearly a year earlier, when we'd collaborated in solving a murder.

I considered him one of my closest friends again, but the line between romance and friendship was a little fuzzy for us. First I'd thought that his high school passion could serve as the basis for a grown-up relationship, but we'd just never seemed to find our way back to that path. Then, when I started dating Jack, he and Sean had become hostile toward each other, acting like romantic rivals. Because we were friends, it wasn't unusual for Sean to stop by at odd hours, sometimes just to chat, but I never knew if he might suddenly decide that we should be—that we *were*—

more than friends. And I had no idea what Jack would think if he knew that Sean and I were hanging out in the wee hours.

"Haven't you been home yet?" His tie was gone, but Sean still wore the suit he'd worn through a day of lawyering.

"No. You wouldn't believe the day I've had."

"Back at you." I handed him his bowl of ice cream.

"I heard you found Denford's body?"

I nodded.

"That must have been horrible for you. Are you okay?"

I froze. No one—not even dear, dear Jack, not even my own mother—had asked if I was okay with what I'd seen. And, frankly, I'd thought I was doing just fine. After all, it was my third body. I should have been used to death by then.

But the moment the words came out of Sean's mouth, I realized I'd been holding my emotions in all day. Yes, I'd seen dead people before, people I'd known better and liked more than Denford. Still, this was different. More brutal. More real. Phillip's murder scene was by far the most viscerally violent scene I'd ever witnessed.

And once Phillip's meeting with me the morning of his death came to light, I might find myself a suspect. There was no question that I couldn't keep my secret forever. . . . Thus far I'd only been staving off the inevitable. I had no idea how anyone—especially Jack—would react when the truth eventually came out.

I felt wobbly inside and could feel tears welling in my eyes.

Sean took the ice cream from my hands and placed both dishes on the counter, then pulled me into his embrace. The sound of his heart thumping beneath my ear made me lose it. I started sobbing in earnest and wrapped my arms tightly around Sean's neck. He held me gently, whispering a steady stream of calming nonsense into my hair.

The storm was hard but quick. I don't know what possessed me, but as my tears subsided, I straightened in Sean's arms, looked him dead in the eye, and kissed him.

It was a nice kiss. No fireworks, no sparks, but a soothing warmth spread through my veins. For his part, Sean stood perfectly still. He didn't lean in to the kiss or hold me tighter, but he didn't step away, either. Rather, I was the one who, after just a few short seconds, jumped back as though I'd been teetering on the soft edge of a cliff.

"Oh God. I'm so, so sorry," I muttered as I wiped the lingering tears from my face. "That was horrible."

"Gee, thanks," Sean said, his lips quirking up in a wry smile.

"Oh, no . . . I didn't mean to . . . Oh heavens. I don't know what I'm doing."

"You're apologizing for kissing me. No apology necessary." I opened my mouth, but he cut me off. "Before you say another word, I know you were overwrought and that you weren't thinking clearly. I won't hold you to it. Let's just pretend it never happened." He was letting me off the hook, but there was an impatient edge to his voice, one that made me feel small, like I was being a drama queen by thinking the event even merited an apology.

For the most part, I was overwhelmingly relieved by his comment. But somewhere in the darkest, most shameful corner of my heart, his reaction stung. He was so matter-of-fact about it. The kiss had been spontaneous on my part, the result of an overabundance of emotion in general rather than emotion about Sean specifically. And I did love Sean as one of my oldest and dearest friends, so I didn't want him to suffer. But his apparent ability to blow it off was a bit of a hit to my ego.

"Well," Sean said, picking his bowl back up, "I've been retained by Pris Olson. So far she's been charged only for the theft, but Jerry in the county attorney's office made it clear they were looking hard at her for the murder, too." He took a bite of his ice cream, and his eyes fluttered shut as he slipped the spoon from between his lips. "Dang. That hits the spot. Anyway, it took all day, but Hal Olson finally convinced Judge Rancik to arraign Pris after hours and set her bail so she could go home tonight. I feel like I've been at the courthouse for a week rather than a single day."

"You must be exhausted."

"Yeah, but I still wanted to see you. Pris is so wound up about the arrest and the indignity of spending hours in a holding cell that she couldn't think straight. The only information I got, I got from the cops and the prosecutors; talking to Pris was like talking to a wall. But I want to do some damage control on this ASAP. I want to point the police in a different direction before they get around to indicting my client for murder. So I wanted to talk to someone who was actually there today, actually at the scene of the crime."

"I don't know what I can tell you. Denford must have been killed sometime before everyone arrived this morning. I mean, his body was in the middle of a crowded room. But the jewels were on display before the lights went out. I'd been admiring Jolly's handiwork not fifteen minutes earlier. It was only after the lights came back on that I noticed they were missing . . . and no one else reported seeing anything amiss before then, either."

"That's helpful. So the murder and the theft weren't committed at the same time. Maybe not even by the same people."

"No one will believe that," I said. "The two crimes

were committed in such physical and temporal proximity, everyone will assume that there's only one perpetrator."

He leaned back against the counter, ankles crossed, and stared into the middle distance for a while. "What about Pris?"

"What about her?"

"Well, was she acting funny this morning?"

"She had some sort of blowout with Phillip yesterday afternoon, but I didn't see her in the ballroom at all this morning. At least, not until the lights came back on. I was a few minutes late to the opening of the show. Rena said she saw Pris before I got there, but by the time I arrived, I couldn't find her anywhere. And I was looking for her, because we had business to discuss. If she was in the ballroom at all before the blackout, she'd left by the time I got there."

"Really? She insists she was in the room, at her station, the whole morning."

"Well, that's weird. Why would she insist she was at the scene of the crime—a statement that makes her look guilty—when I'm mighty sure she was gone?"

"Her being gone when you got to the ballroom doesn't exactly get her off the hook, especially if Phillip was killed before the masses started showing up this morning. But still, you're right that she'd want to distance herself as much as possible from the location, if only to provide an alibi for the theft of the dangle."

"I feel like I know Pris pretty well, but I don't always understand why she does the things she does. The woman moves in mysterious ways."

"Well, you certainly know Pris a lot better than I do. Is she capable of these crimes?"

"Rena made a pretty good case at dinner that the crimes aren't Pris's style. She's more subtle. She would have found a way to embezzle money from someone, or helped Hal with one of his many scams, rather than steal an actual thing out from under everyone's noses. But Pris has been under pressure lately, and so who knows?"

"But does she have it in her to break the law? Ignoring how the crimes were committed, does she have it in her to steal and kill?"

"There are times when I actually enjoy Pris's company, but I'm always aware that her moral compass is a bit askew. Under the right circumstances, I could see her as a killer."

Sean sighed. "Yeah, that's the impression I got, too. And whatever happens, I can't let her get in front of a jury. She's so . . . so . . ."

"Superior? Dismissive? Snide?" I offered.

He laughed. "Yes. That. All of that."

"Listen," I said, "I know our friendship took a real blow that night of the storm." The night an eighteen-year-old Sean Tucker pledged his love to me and begged me to dump my boyfriend. The night I shot him down and told him I didn't love him. The night he rode his bike off into the darkness and the rain and commenced a fifteen-year stretch of silence between us.

"It did," he conceded.

"But we're still friends, right? We've gotten past that bitterness?"

He blinked, considering. "I'm not sure I'll ever be totally past that, Izzy, but yes, we're still friends."

I sighed in relief. "Then I have a major favor to ask. As your friend. If you haven't really talked with Pris about the theft and the murder, could you still back out of representing her?"

Sean tilted his head to one side, brow furrowed in puzzlement. "I suppose so. In fact, I have a fairly full schedule these days and was thinking of referring her to my friend Rudy over in Wild Rapids. He's got more experience working murder cases, and he wouldn't be going into the case with the baggage of actually knowing Pris."

"You mean he doesn't already think she's shady?"

Sean smiled. "I wouldn't go quite that far, but I certainly know Hal and I don't hold him in particularly high esteem. I'd like to think I'm a professional and could give Pris zealous representation no matter what my preexisting thoughts about her and her spouse may be, but why risk it?"

"Thank you."

"Like I said, I'm not really doing it for you, though

I'm glad the decision makes you happy. But why would you want me to give up representing Pris? What difference does it make to you?"

"Because, before this is all over, I may need your services more."

CHAPTER
Seven

Rena and I arrived at the show bright and early the following morning. Once again, Jinx did her turn as fashion model while wearing hot-pink neck and mitt ruffs. The effect was a sort of seventies bell-bottoms-and-poncho look, and the hot pink set off my big girl's black-and-white fur to perfection. Since she clocked in at nearly twenty pounds, I had her set up in a crate for medium-sized dogs because cat kennels were just too cramped for her to spend an entire day in.

I'd had Jinx for several years, having surprised myself by adopting her at an event at the Merryville mall. As she'd aged, she'd started slowing down, her body becoming more lean. Still the cat had swagger. She looked at me through the bars of the kennel, and

I could swear I saw her wink at me. Unlike many cats who get skittish around strangers, Jinx lapped up the attention like sweet cream.

Rena offered to man our stall for the morning while I wandered the show a bit, trying to locate Gandhi. I took a handful of our cards to hand out as I hunted.

I made a complete circuit around the ballroom, watching the fanciers tending their furry charges and scanning the floor for a glimpse of Gandhi. I couldn't decide whether I hoped he was in the room with all the cats—where he was prey, but where I might actually find him—or that he had escaped into some other part of the hotel—where he would be on his own, a life that seemed to work for him, until some disgruntled guest or health inspector got the little guy exterminated.

I'd finished a lap of the room, with one potential guinea pig sighting (it turned out to be a plush cat toy), and was on my way back to our booth, when someone tapped me on the arm.

"I remember you." I turned to find I had just passed the outspoken woman from yesterday's crime scene, the woman with the wire-rimmed glasses and the cribbage board. "You were the one who found Phillip's body."

"How do you—?"

"Know so much about what happened?" she finished for me. "Well, my table is right there." She pointed to a table at the end of the row, just one in from the aisle where we'd set up the Trendy Tails booth. "And I pay attention."

Hmmm. I wondered whether other people might refer to her "paying attention" as "meddling."

I extended my hand, happy to welcome a kindred spirit. "Izzy—"

"McHale. Yes, I know. You design the cat clothes."

"And dog clothes."

She blinked at me like I'd suddenly started speaking another language.

Finally, she took my hand. A bracelet hung from her birdlike wrist, tinkling with charms shaped like hearts and cats. "Ruth Kimmey."

"It's nice to meet you, Ruth. Which of these beautiful babies is yours?"

I followed Ruth the handful of steps to her station. Her kennel was made of black wire and draped with faux leopard fur. Inside, an oval cat bed exploded with fur the color and texture of dandelion fluff. As I bent down to examine more closely, the fluff rippled gently and one baleful blue eye popped open and latched onto me.

"Gorgeous," I said.

"He is, isn't he? This is Cataclysm Ranger."

"Cataclysm?"

Ruth cocked her head and studied me curiously. "Do you know much about cat shows, Izzy?"

I shrugged one shoulder. "Not much," I conceded.

"I'm sure some of my customers show their animals, but it's not something that comes up in our conversations over fashion."

"Well, let me bring you up to speed. I love to share my love of cats with others. Show animals are known by their mother's cattery—in Ranger's case, his mama was from a cattery in Iowa called Cataclysm. He's a peke-faced sterling Persian."

"A what-what?"

"Peke-faced means his profile is vertical, without a muzzle sticking out to ruin the line. Sterling means his fur is white with just the very tips shaded in gray. That's what makes him sparkle like that."

"Interesting."

"Ranger is a grand premier. He's actually racked up enough wins that he'd be a grand champion if my son-of-a-gun ex-husband hadn't had him neutered. He's nearly flawless. Just a hint of tarnishing around his nose."

One thing I'd learned during my days of planning for the cat show is that unaltered cats competed for champion and grand-champion status while neutered males could only achieve the status of grand premier.

As the cat lifted its head and opened both eyes I could see just the faintest hint of yellowing in the fur between Ranger's nose and upper lip. If Ruth hadn't pointed it out, I wouldn't have noticed.

"You can barely see that," I said.

Ruth shrugged. "The judges are paid to see that. Even when I use Ducky White on his muzzle, the judges seem to spot it."

"Ducky White?"

"It's a coat chalk. My personal favorite. It's used to whiten the coat and absorb any stray oil on the cat. Like I said, it hides Ranger's tarnish well, but not quite well enough. He more than makes up for that coat flaw with his straight back and perfect little cobby body. He also shows well. His temperament is perfect. When he's in the judging ring, being handled by the judge, he's alert but still. And when the judge brings out a toy, he sits up on his back legs, showing off his body structure, and reaches up and out to bat at the toy so he doesn't block his beautiful face. He nails it every time."

"Wow." I studied the giant fluff ball in the crate. Jinx was a long-haired breed, and her fur was winter-ready plush, but it was nowhere near as full and dense as Ranger's. I thought about how much time I spent combing out Jinxie's lovely locks. "What does it take to keep Ranger's fur so nice?"

"Daily comb-outs to start. Then, the day before the show, Ranger gets a full bath: four lathers with complete rinses between each, then a blowout, followed by a bit of grooming just to make sure his coat is perfectly symmetrical: ear tufts, whiskers, and eyebrows. Day of the show, I comb through the Ducky White to freshen him up and try to cover that tarnishing a bit."

"So that's what Pris would have done? The full bath?"

"If I trusted a stranger with my Ranger, then yes. But I don't. I always groom him myself, tip to tail. Though I seem to have forgotten my grooming kit, so that criminal will get some money out of me before the day is done. Or, at least, her business will."

That criminal. Poor Pris. We'd both been hoping that this show would help our businesses really take off. I'd hoped to gain some more Internet business, and Pris had hoped that she could secure invitations to other M-CFO events where she could set up mobile grooming stations. But with the cat fanciers referring to Pris as "that criminal" instead of "that groomer," I feared she—and Prissy's Pretty Pets—might be doomed.

"I won't be happy about it, though," she continued. "Pris doesn't carry my brand of grooming shears. I only use Guttenheim shears. The kind that Mr. Denford sells on his Classy Cat Web site."

Ruth reached a finger through the bars of Ranger's kennel and stroked the area beneath his mouth, what would have been his neck if Persians had real necks.

"I'm surprised you're not out watching the agility show. Ranger here only does conformation judging; I wouldn't risk him getting grimy or falling on the agility course. But it is wildly entertaining to watch."

Ruth beckoned to a statuesque woman in a crystal-studded leopard tracksuit, her hair bleached beyond blond, her eye makeup more appropriate for a cabaret than a cat show. I recognized her as the breeder who'd gotten into a tizzy about her tabby's markings on the day before the show was scheduled to start. She'd been in head-to-toe leopard then, too. Apparently, she had a very distinct sense of style.

The woman squeed and rushed to our side, a happy little waggle in her walk.

"Izzy, this is T. J. Leuzinger, owner of Cataclysm Cattery. T.J., Izzy owns Trendy Tails, the pet boutique here in town."

T.J. reached out and grasped one of my hands in both of her bejeweled mitts. Her hands smelled like coconut.

"So great to meet you, Izzy. I've seen some of your designs in the showroom. You're quite a hit."

Her comment did my heart good.

"T.J., could you watch Ranger for a bit? I don't want to leave him alone, but Izzy here's never seen a cat-agility competition so I want to show her what we do."

"Of course. Be happy to. I haven't had a chance to get caught up with this handsome fella in quite a while."

We left T.J. making cooing sounds to Ranger as Ruth led me out the side door of the North Woods Hotel and into a giant parklike setting. Although you could hear cars passing by, lilac bushes blocked the green space from any view of Beechnut Road. In the distance, I spotted a gazebo where many a Merryville wedding had taken place. Closer, though, a generous white tent had been set up about fifty feet from the door. A huge crush of people gathered tight around the perimeter of the tent. From the cheering, I guessed that the agility show was already in progress.

Despite the crowd, Ruth managed to strong-arm her way to the front, securing the two of us spaces to stand just outside the velvet rope that marked off the course. I felt guilty about both our barging and my height, so I crouched down a little for the people behind me.

I quickly took in the lay of the land. The agility course had been "carpeted" with a cheap green Astroturf, likely to protect the tender pads on the cats' paws from dirt and rocks. At one corner of the course, a pudgy man in jeans and a "Cats Rule, Dogs Drool" T-shirt was getting a lean Russian blue situated to start.

"In case you were wondering," Ruth said quietly, subtly pointing her pinkie toward the judging table, "Pamela Rawlins is not a fan of agility. She's a conformation snob." Pamela sat at a small table, wedged between Mari Aames and Marsha Denford, her pitch hair glistening in the bright August sunlight. None of the women appeared particularly happy to be there, but Pamela's face was set in an obvious pout.

"My gracious," I said, "how can three women manage to have their backs to one another while still sitting in a straight line?"

Ruth hooted. "You got that right. Those ladies would literally bend over backward to avoid one another."

"Why? They were all clustered together like baby chicks yesterday while the police were processing the crime scene. There was plenty of space in the ballroom, even with the taped-off bit. I assumed they must have wanted to be together."

"Oh, sure," Ruth said. "But I don't think they were offering one another sympathy. I think they were each keeping an eye on the other two. See, all three of them wanted a piece of Phillip Denford, and there just wasn't enough of Phillip to go around."

"Really?" I prodded.

"Absolutely. Marsha and Mari have been at it for years. Marsha needs Phillip so she can be Marsha Denford and Mari needs Phillip so she has a job. Each sees the other as a threat. Then, last year, there was a rumor that Denford and Pamela had had a little fling. This, of course, did not make Marsha happy. I don't know whether she was genuinely hurt by the affair or just embarrassed by it, but either way she's given Pamela the cold shoulder ever since. And Pamela pushed her way into acting as cocoordinator of this silver-anniversary event, edging Mari farther to the side and threatening her job. I'm not sure what Pamela wanted out of the whole deal—if she was happy playing a bigger role in the M-CFO or if she saw herself as some genuine love interest—but Phillip definitely planned to placate her with the event coordinator title . . . Even then, it was just a title. Mari's still the one who did all the heavy lifting."

"It all sounds so . . . complicated."

Ruth laughed again. "This is nothing compared to the old days. The world of cat shows, or at least those sponsored by the Midwest Cat Fanciers' Organization, has always been a hotbed of intrigue. I have to admit that the murder takes things to a whole new level, but it's still tame compared to the days of off-the-books kitten swapping and key parties."

I tried to imagine mousy-looking diminutive Ruth Kimmey, garbed in a cat sweatshirt, tossing her keys into a bowl, and I just couldn't get there.

"Oh, he's ready to start," she said. "This should be good. That's Jeffrey Brockman. Some people call him 'the cat whisperer,' because he can get his animals to perform the most amazing feats of agility on courses far more difficult than this."

Sure enough, the man with the Russian blue was standing on his tiptoes, a cat dancer toy in one hand. A bell rang, and he started to trot along the side of the course, leading the cat with the wand. The blue ran up a ramp, then down the other side, made its way through nylon tunnels that curved in gentle arcs, slithered its way through a slalom of orange cones, and then did a graceful leap over a low hurdle. As he landed, though, his tail caught the crossbar of the hurdle and knocked it off. The whole crowd gasped.

Ruth moaned softly. "Too bad. Ivan was a favorite for the course. His time was great, but there will be a deduction for knocking off the crossbar. Jeffrey must be crushed."

It was true. Even across the tent, I could see the expression on Jeffrey's face. He was stroking Ivan gently, letting the cat nibble treats from his hand, but he looked distraught.

For some reason it struck me hard as I took in the sense of longing and loss in Jeffrey's expression: other than Mari Aames, no one had looked even half so devastated upon learning of Phillip Denford's demise.

Jack brought Rena and me lunch that day, toasted cheese sandwiches wrapped in wax paper, creamy tomato soup in a thermos, and a half-dozen tea cookies from my friend Taffy's Happy Leaf Tea Shoppe.

"Any luck finding Gandhi?" he asked as he handed over the canvas lunch bag, a teasing smile gracing his lips. I'd filled him in on our tiny escape artist's newest trick: a rodent navigating a room filled with cats.

"Not yet. Any luck finding Phillip's killer?"

He glared at me and shook his head. "Look. I realize the evidence so far is circumstantial, but all of it points to Pris. We know she had a fight with Phillip the day before he died. We know she had access to the type of tool used to kill the man. And we know that she stole the jeweled collar piece."

"Dangle."

He sighed. "Dangle."

"But how do you know that the theft and the murder are related?"

"We don't know for sure, but the odds of these two major crimes being committed so close together but by different people? They're pretty slim."

"It's possible, though."

"Yes, anything's possible."

"It's just that I can maybe imagine Pris stealing, especially given her current financial situation, but the murder doesn't fit. And if you look at the crimes as two separate incidents, it changes the scope of the possible suspects."

"Trust me when I tell you that the police are exploring every option."

The tone of his voice told me it was time to move on. Jack was done talking about the cat-show crime spree.

"Have you taken a look around the show yet?"

"Not really. I'd just arrived yesterday morning when you found Phillip's body. The techs wandered around the ballroom a bit, but I was stuck taking statements." He looked around. "Tell me all about it."

"It's absolutely fascinating. There are nine judging rings." I pointed out the spaces around the perimeter of the room, each with a bank of empty kennels behind it and a long folding table at its front. "There's a judge for each ring, and each judge sees all the breed groupings, one at a time. Except for the household-pet category. Those cats get seen by only a single judge."

"Household pet?"

"Yeah. If you have a cat that you think is pretty special but it doesn't have pedigree papers, you can still show him off in the household-pet division. That's near the end of the show. I can't wait."

Jack tore a corner from my cheese sandwich and popped it in his mouth.

"Hey!"

He shrugged. "I brought you lemon cookies to make up for it." This man knew the way to my heart. Taffy's lemon cookies erased a multitude of sins. "Did you think about entering Jinx in the show?"

I dropped my head down to get a better look at my gorgeous girl showing off a Fair Isle sweater-vest. "I thought about it when I heard about the pet category, but I figured I didn't know that much about showing and, while Jinx is a good-natured cat, I wasn't sure how she'd hold up to being picked up and prodded by strangers."

As I stood back up, I realized that a crowd was gathering around one of the judging rings. "Oh! Let's go watch."

I tucked my sandwich back in its waxed-paper wrapping and dragged Jack by the hand to the judging ring. The judge, a middle-aged man with a pale blond comb-over, was moving from cage to cage to get an overall impression of the animals while his clerk shuffled the ballots. The grouping appeared to be exotic short hairs.

"What's that?"

"They're crosses between American short hairs and exotics like Persians, Burmese, and Russian blues."

"They just look like cats to me," Jack muttered.

I elbowed him in the ribs.

The judge removed a cat from its kennel and announced its name—Tigerbrite Lex—and set it on the table. First the judge ran his hands over the cat, then peered into its broad, flat face. He picked up a cat dancer toy and engaged the animal to see the way it moved and how alert it was. Finally, he picked the cat up, one hand under its front legs and the other under its back legs, holding him almost like a fat, furry rifle, and swiveled the cat around for all of us to see. He made a few comments about the cat's lovely coloring and clear eyes, then whispered more comments to the clerk, who was filling out the ballots.

The judge repeated this act with each of the cats. When he was done with the final cat, he chatted with the clerk one last time, picked up a handful of ribbons, and began sticking them to the kennels seemingly at random. There were gasps and *ooh*s from the audience, who apparently understood the significance of all the ribbons better than I did.

Jack and I left the ring quickly, before there was a mad rush to return all the cats to their individual kennels, and headed back to the Trendy Tails booth.

"I guess I don't get why people do this," Jack said.

"What do you mean?"

"Why do people care what other people think of their pets?"

I shrugged. "Why do people enter their big hogs in the state fair?"

"That's different," Jack asserted. "A hog is worth more if it weighs more. A pet's a pet whether it's pretty or not. People are supposed to love their pets, right? No matter what they look like?"

My heart went pitter-patter.

"Yes, but everyone thinks that their cat is the best, the prettiest, the most perfect animal out there. Something special. I guess cat shows are a way for people to prove that their babies are special. When you were younger, didn't you tell everyone stories about how smart your dog was or how sweet your cat was?"

"I never had a cat or a dog. Or any pet, for that matter."

"You've never had a pet? How is that possible?"

Jack shrugged, sending muscles rippling every which way beneath his well-fitting T-shirt. "When I was growing up, Mom and Dad both had jobs. They could barely juggle taking care of me. A pet was out of the question. And then, well, I was used to being petless. I never noticed there might be something missing in my life until Mom adopted Pearl after Dad died."

"You've spent a lot of time with Pearl. I remember your mom saying that you'd gone on walks and runs with Pearl to help her slim down to a healthier weight." Pearl, an elderly beagle, had been found behind a bakery, where she'd apparently subsisted on jelly doughnuts and day-old pie. She'd been positively rotund when Louise Collins brought her in from the cold.

"I did. And that was just fine. But it's not the same as having something of my own. When Pearl and I get back from our little jogs, she runs straight to Mom. I'm just a playdate."

I reached out to take his hand. "Do you want a dog? I could see you with an Australian shepherd, or maybe an English bulldog."

He squeezed my fingers briefly, then ducked his head.

"Despite all this nonsense"—he waved his hand to indicate the ballroom around us—"I think I may be more of a cat person," he muttered.

"A cat person? Really?"

His face flushed a dull crimson. "Yes."

I couldn't stop the bubble of laughter that escaped my lips.

He tugged his hand away from mine. "I know. I know. Big guy like me ought to have a manly pet. I shouldn't have said anything."

"Oh no," I squeaked, trying to recapture both his hand and my composure. "I'm not laughing at you."

He met my gaze and cocked an eyebrow.

Another giggle tumbled out. "Okay, fair enough. But I'm not laughing about you being a cat person. I'm laughing because you're so embarrassed to want a kitten. Lots of really tough guys dig cats. You know, there are whole Web sites devoted to pictures of heavy-metal musicians with their cats."

"Really? That's weird."

Come to think of it, he was right. It was weird. But that wasn't the point. "If you want a cat, I know just where to go. In the back corner of the cat-show floor, the Brainerd shelter has a table with cats up for adoption." I clasped his hand tighter and tugged him along behind me as we once again traversed the sea of cat and humanity in the ballroom.

The Brainerd Animal Rescue occupied two tables

in the back of the ballroom. In one crate they housed two adult cats, both exotic long-haired breeds. In the other . . . kittens. I counted five, but it was difficult to untangle the mess of legs and heads as they wrestled with one another. Finally, in the back of the kitten cage, an adult marmalade tabby quietly watched the kitten antics.

"That's Jingles," the woman manning the station said. "He's about a year old, so he still might grow a bit." That was saying something, because Jingles was already a great big boy.

"Jingles?" I asked. The name didn't match the cat.

The woman chuckled. "When he first came to us, he was a scrawny stray, barely weaned. The name made more sense then."

"You've had him that long?" Jack asked.

"Not exactly. He was adopted as a kitten, but his family moved and couldn't take him with them, so they brought him back. He's been pretty sanguine about it. He's a mellow dude. Want to hold him?"

"Can we?"

The woman opened the cage and reached past the brawling kittens to pull Jingles out. She handed him to me, and for a moment I delighted in his warm, heavy body and rumbling purr, but then I passed him along to Jack.

He held the cat gingerly at first, shifting the cat around as he tried to figure out the best way to hold him. Finally, he opted for holding the tabby like a baby, cradled in his arms and tummy up. Jingles's purr revved up a notch or two.

"Hey, buddy," Jack murmured.

The sight of my strapping boyfriend cuddling this wee beastie in his arms twisted something inside of me, shifting something I didn't even know was out of place into its proper alignment.

And it was clearly love at first cuddle with Jack and Jingles. I could see the tension slip from his shoulders and the crinkles at the corners of his eyes deepen.

"Do you want to take him?" I whispered.

He chucked Jingles under the chin. "What do you say, little man? You want to come live with me? I promise we'll find a more butch name for you."

Both the woman from the shelter and I laughed. "I don't know," I said. "Jack and Jingles has a certain ring to it."

He frowned down at the cat. "Nah. He looks like more of a Steve to me. Simple, strong. Isn't that right, little man?"

I caught the shelter woman's eyes. "I think we're taking this cat."

CHAPTER
Eight

As soon as we were able to shut down the Trendy Tails stall at the cat show, I sent Rena back to Maple Avenue to help Wanda take care of any spillover customers and then close up the shop. Wanda was only seventeen and I didn't like her being at the store alone in the evenings . . . even if it was still light outside.

I jumped in my eight-year-old Honda and drove out to Quail Run, the posh housing development where all the Merryville elite dwelled. Pris Olson had once been the reigning queen of Quail Run, owning the largest of the large lots and the biggest of the big houses. But lately, despite her husband's rise to the seat of mayor of Merryville, Pris had become the local Cinderella. I felt bad for her, knowing how much prestige meant to Pris. Still, it was hard to feel *too* bad for her when I parked my old but serviceable car behind her midnight-blue Mercedes.

I hoisted myself out of my car and approached the wide, ornately carved double doors. The bell played a stately chime, the sort of note progression used by grandfather clocks and bell towers. It used to play Beethoven's Fifth, and I wondered momentarily why Pris and Hal had changed it.

Pris herself opened the door, her cat, Kiki, draped over one shoulder. Kiki lifted her hugely furry head from Pris's shoulder and hissed at me. For reasons only the cat understood, Kiki had never liked me.

"Dear God, Izzy. I really don't want to talk business right now. I've got more than enough to worry about."

"I didn't come about business—though, now that you mention it, just give me a yell if you need any help at the cat show. Rena and I are happy to pitch in."

Pris took a step outside, scanning the street as though someone might be watching our exchange. "Come in," she commanded.

Entering the Olson house was like stepping into the pages of *Architectural Digest*. The travertine tiles of the palatial entryway were topped with a traditional burgundy and ecru Oriental carpet, gold-framed mirrors flanked the entryway into the überbeige formal living room, and the light from the crystal chandelier picked up the hints of gold in the ivory damask wallpaper. I didn't see any personal items at all. We could have been standing in the foyer of a model home.

Pris fit here perfectly, but I had a hard time imagining her husband in this environment. Hal Olson was a big, blustery man, a former football player sliding from muscle to fat as he aged. Sun and wind had pickled his skin to a permanent ruddy tan, and he tended to lead with his head when he walked. I could imagine Hal enjoying a mile-high cold-cut sandwich dripping with Russian dressing, but I couldn't imagine him enjoying it in this house.

"Thanks for the offer," Pris said, "but I think my girls can handle everything. I just made them promise they wouldn't let Dee Dee Lahti touch the money. Or interact with customers. I mean, I feel sorry for the woman, but I'm not stupid."

"Well, if anything comes up."

"Will do." Her features softened. "Really. Thank you."

"Of course," I said. I scuffed the toe of my sneaker against the tile and shoved my hands in the pockets of my jeans. Her sincerity made me uncomfortable.

"Well, if you didn't come to talk business, what brings you all the way out to Quail Run?"

There was no point beating around the bush. "I wanted to talk to you about the collar dangle and Phillip Denford."

All hint of softness fled as Pris's face hardened into an enamel mask.

"And why on earth would I talk to you about any of that?"

"Because I don't think you did anything wrong. Because, from what I've heard, you don't have many people to confide in anymore." I took a deep breath. "And because I'm determined to find out who the real perpetrator is."

She rolled her eyes. "You and your wacky pack are planning to solve another murder?"

"You have to admit we have a pretty good track record."

Pris laughed, and some of the tension drained from her posture.

"I don't understand why you're interested in helping me. Sean Tucker dumped me, so now I have to go out of town to find a decent criminal lawyer, and I suspect you had something to do with that. So far it looks like you're doing your best to see me convicted."

I shook my head. "Absolutely not. The thing with Sean is . . . complicated. And didn't he recommend someone in Wild Rapids to represent you?"

"He did. And the new attorney has quite a solid pedigree. But I'm puzzled why Sean wouldn't want the case for himself, and I tend to think he gave it up because you asked him to. Which raises the question of why you would care about who my attorney is. Only answer I can come up with is that you want to throw me under the bus."

I know I was trying to get Pris to spill her guts to me, but I didn't want to tell her about my glaring motive if I didn't have to. It just wouldn't be prudent. "Trust me when I say that I'm as motivated to find the real killer as you are."

"And what makes you so certain it wasn't me? Do you think I couldn't kill someone?"

"Oh no. I think if you were pushed hard enough, you would absolutely kill someone."

Pris laughed. "I'm glad you have such a high opinion of my character."

I could feel myself blushing. "It's not a criticism. Believe me, if there's one thing I've learned over the last year, it's that just about anyone can be pushed to kill. But I don't believe you killed Phillip Denford because I saw the body. Lots of blood. If you wanted to kill someone, you would poison them. Maybe shoot them. But you wouldn't get all up close and personal and get blood on yourself."

"Excellent point," Pris purred as she ushered me into the formal living room. All of the furniture was in shades of white and ecru with only the occasional pop of burgundy from a potted plant or a throw pillow. The vaulted ceiling made the room feel like the set of a movie, not a place actual where people lived.

At Pris's direction, I sat on one of the ivory sofas. I perched on the edge of the cushion, self-conscious about the possibility of getting fur or dust on the pristine seat.

Pris sat in an oversized armchair, a veritable throne. A low mahogany table with gently curved Queen Anne legs separated us.

"So what can I tell you?" Pris asked. "What magic bit of information is going to help you clear my name?"

"I don't entirely know. But it would help to know what the police think happened."

"Your boyfriend hasn't told you already? No crime-fighting pillow talk?"

Once again, my cheeks burned. "No. Jack's official line is that it's an ongoing investigation. I think he's keeping mum for more personal reasons, though. He really doesn't want me involved, so he hasn't shared any of the good stuff with me."

"Aha. He's trying to rein in the inquisitive Izzy McHale. He's a brave man."

"Yeah. I guess he is. But will *you* tell me what the police think happened?"

"Why not? It can't really hurt me any more than that stupid collar dangle did."

She leaned back, slipping off her ballet flats and curling her toes around the top of the coffee table. I'd never seen Pris so relaxed and casual.

"They said that Phillip was killed early that morning. By the time you found him, he'd been dead at least a couple of hours, so he wasn't killed during the blackout. Their theory is that Phillip and I arrived early. We relived our fight from the afternoon before. I grabbed a pair of my grooming shears and stabbed him while he was standing close to the prize table, then shoved his body under the table."

"By yourself."

"Yep. Then, since I would have been covered in blood, I managed to get to my car without anyone seeing me, drive home, change, and get back to the show in time for the official opening at nine."

"Okay. What about the theft?"

"Again, I'm apparently quite clever. And speedy. I managed to slip out of the ballroom and throw the breakers on the lights, slip back in through the door by my stall, make my way through the pitch-black to the prize table, grab the jewels, and get back to my stall before the lights came back on."

"Really?"

"Really."

I shook my head. "No offense, but that sounds pretty complicated."

Pris narrowed her eyes. "I think I'm smart enough to have come up with the plan, Izzy. But there's no way I had time to do all that. The lights were out for only a few minutes before Jack managed to prop open the front door and shed light on the inside of the ball-room. I was back by my stall in the corner during the entire blackout."

"Actually *in* your stall?"

"No. I was out front."

"But I looked everywhere for you and couldn't find you. I didn't see you at all until a good hour after the lights came back on. If you weren't even in the room that morning, you should tell the police. If you weren't there, you couldn't have stolen the dangle. I'll back you up."

Pris's lips thinned. "Well, that would be lovely. But I *was* there. You must have missed me. Right before the lights went out, I'd been talking to this kind of crusty old broad. Gray fuzzy hair, wire-rimmed glasses—the one who offered to play cribbage while the police investigated the crime scene."

"Ruth Kimmey."

"Right. Ruth. We'd been talking about how sad it was that Pamela Rawlins wouldn't be involved with organizing the shows in the future. Frankly, I'm not sorry at all. I don't like that Pamela woman very much. She's a little snooty."

Said the pot to the kettle.

"Next year, Marsha Denford will be in charge."

"I thought Phillip was the one associated with the M-CFO."

"He was. But it's like a dynasty, and Marsha is next

in line. She'll carry on Phillip's tradition of coordinating the show. At least, she'll be the figurehead over the whole enchilada. Assuming Marsha keeps her on, Mari will probably still be stuck handling the details. But it's great for me. Marsha and I get along brilliantly. Assuming I'm not in prison, I should be in a great position for next year's show."

"Did you tell the police all this?"

"Are you kidding? I know enough to keep my mouth shut when it comes to the police. I didn't say a word."

"Pris, I have to say you're very calm about your situation. I'd be losing my mind."

She reached up a hand to smooth her hair. "I'm innocent. I have to believe that means something. And, besides, I'm following the advice of counsel to the letter. Before he severed his representation, Sean said I did exactly the right thing by keeping mum about Pamela's ouster from the M-CFO planning committee. 'Don't ever talk to the cops,' he said. 'Not ever. Even if you're telling them something that may seem to help you, it could come back to bite you later.'"

I understood why Pris, as a prime suspect, would want to keep quiet, but I was dating the cops. While I might someday come to regret it, I had no choice but to speak with them. Besides, the more I thought about it, the more I realized I had to come clean with Jack.

Not only was it the right thing to do for our relationship, but I was pretty sure I was Pris's alibi.

I met with Jack that night at his place.

He lived in the second-floor apartment of an old Victorian house, just a few blocks down Maple from Trendy Tails. It was spacious but sparsely furnished. Jack wasn't a complicated guy. He needed a comfy couch and a good TV, not a lot of bric-a-brac and fancy paintings on the wall. In fact, the only decoration on his walls was a series of framed family photos taken by his uncle Paul. They were good black-and-white photos, but they were nothing arty or pretentious. My favorite was a close-up of his mother, Louise, and her fat beagle, Pearl, both grinning at the camera.

I walked in and was instantly enveloped by the pungent scent of cilantro and the piquant bite of jalapeños. Shortly after we'd begun dating, I'd discovered Jack's hidden passion for cooking.

"Salsa?" It was one of his specialties, a complex blend of roasted chilies brightened with fresh lime juice and herbs.

"Yeah," he called from the kitchen. "Just finished a batch. I'll be right out."

I made myself at home on the canvas sofa, pulling a squishy velvet pillow from between the cushions and pressing it to my chest. I scanned the living room floor, taking in the cat toys strewn every which way.

"Are you and Steve getting situated?"

"Absolutely. The minute I set him down in the apartment, he went on patrol, checking out every room, before jumping up on my bed, rolling onto his back, and conking out. He's right at home. And thanks for all the toys. He's a big fan. As a cop, I shouldn't approve, but the little guy likes to get high on the 'nip."

I laughed. "Where is he now?"

"Probably passed out on the bed." Jack emerged from the kitchen with a big basket of tortilla chips and a dish of his salsa, both of which he set on the coffee table in front of the couch. "But, see, I've already got a couple of great pictures."

He handed me his phone, and I scrolled through shots of Steve pouncing on toys, sleeping with his paws curled beneath his chin, and even a selfie of Jack with the cat stretched out next to him. It looked like Steve had quietly fallen into a very sweet gig with a human who was eager to shower love on the little guy.

He'd look great in a little black kitty-hoodie. I suspected that Jack would balk at first, but eventually I would get my way. Eventually, I was going to have fun dressing Steve.

I grabbed a chip and scooped up some of the chunky salsa. After savoring that first bite, I got down to business. "I just got back from talking to Pris."

Jack groaned and rubbed his face with his hands.

"Izzy, I thought we'd been clear about this. Listening is okay, but actual investigation is off-limits."

I rolled my eyes. "It's a fine line."

"Not so fine."

"Whatever. Just hear me out. This is important."

He leaned back against the cushions, angling his body so he could see me sitting next to him without craning his neck. "Okay. Shoot."

"There's no way Pris killed Phillip Denford."

"Uh-huh. And you know this because . . . ?"

"Because I'm her alibi."

He sat up straight. "You were with Pris yesterday morning?"

And this was where things got tricky. "No. I was with Phillip."

He frowned and opened his mouth, but I cut him off with a wave of my hand.

"Pris said you guys think that she met Phillip at the ballroom, killed him before anyone else arrived, stashed his body, went home to change, and got back by nine. But the timing doesn't work. Quail Run is on the opposite side of town from the hotel. It's easily a twenty-minute drive. That's forty minutes round-trip, plus a good ten minutes for Pris to clean up at home and get all done up the way Pris does. That means Pris had to have killed Phillip and left the hotel by ten after eight."

"Okay."

"But at eight yesterday morning, Phillip was at Trendy Tails with me. So that leaves ten minutes for him to get back to the North Woods Hotel, get in a fight with Pris, get himself killed, and for Pris to shove his body underneath the table. It's just not enough time."

I'd spilled my story quickly, the words tumbling over one another in a torrent. When I finished, the sudden silence felt tense.

Steve chose that moment to come into the living room to see what the fuss was about. He rolled his big shoulders as he walked, giving him a gait like a tiger's. But as soon as he made a pass by Jack, rubbing the length of his body along Jack's leg, he found a felt bird filled with catnip. He held it between his front paws and—following thousands of years of genetic wiring— tried to gut it with his back feet.

Jack paid no attention to Steve. He just stared at me for a few minutes. I could see the muscles in his jaw working.

"Maybe Pris got to the show late. We haven't finished corroborating her story."

"No. Rena saw her right before the show opened at nine. She was on time. And, in fact, I was looking for her before the lights went out and that's when she was gone . . . when you all think she was stealing the collar dangle."

"Maybe you didn't see her, but that doesn't mean

she wasn't there," Jack said. "Still, this does change things. What, may I ask, was Phillip doing at your place at eight in the morning yesterday?"

This was the bit I'd really been dreading.

"He was threatening to ruin my business."

Jack sighed and scrubbed his hands over his face again. I might have been giving him a migraine.

"For crying out loud, Izzy. What do you mean?"

"He's started making knockoffs of the clothes I design. He's got a huge Web presence, and he can produce the clothes way cheaper than I can. I don't know how legal it all is, but I can hardly afford a protracted court battle with the man."

"Why didn't you tell me this yesterday? This is important information."

I stared down at the pillow clutched in my lap. The piping around its edges was fraying. If I was still dating Jack at Christmas, I'd make him new covers.

"I didn't want you to think I killed Phillip."

"I don't think you killed anyone," he replied without so much as a heartbeat of a pause.

I looked up through my lashes to find him studying my face. "I could never think anything like that." He reached out to lay a hand over mine.

I flipped my own hand over so I could clasp his fingers and squeeze. "I was afraid. Despite what you may think, I've had enough of murder to last me my entire life. I have no desire to be wrapped up in another killing. And I really don't want to be arrested for one."

"Dang it, Izzy. I love you, but you're killing me."

"What?"

"I said, you're killing me. I want to protect you. I want to keep you out of this whole mess. But I can't just pretend this conversation never happened. I have to tell my colleagues. Your information is critical to the timeline of the crime, but it also makes you a suspect. I mean, I know you didn't kill anyone, but you'll still be a suspect."

I waved off his explanation. "No. Did you say you loved me?"

He froze, a look of shock on his face. "I . . ." He frowned, then shrugged. "Yes. Yes, I did." The challenge in his voice was almost palpable.

"Is that true?" I felt warmth blossoming in my chest.

"I don't lie." Typical Jack response.

"Oh."

"Is that okay?" It was the first time I'd heard real doubt in his voice.

I launched myself at him, throwing my arms around his neck. "Okay? Of course it's okay. It's amazing."

He wrapped his arms around me, squeezing tight, then pulled back so he could look in my eyes.

"You took me by surprise, Izzy McHale. At first I thought I'd just go on a couple of dates with a pretty girl. But there's something about you, like this purity in your soul or something. I can't describe it, but it's addictive."

It was on the tip of my tongue to echo his proclamation back to him. The words gathered in the back of my throat—*I love you, too!*—but being dumped by Casey Alter had burned me badly, and the words couldn't quite get past the scar tissue. I gazed up at him, praying he saw the intensity in my eyes. Finally, I leaned in to plant a series of quick kisses on his lips. "You. Are. The. Best," I pronounced between pecks.

"Yeah, well, 'the best' has to go call Gil Dixon about bringing you in for questioning." Gil Dixon was Jack's partner in crime-solving, another member of Merryville's finest.

His words definitely killed the mood. And as I leaned back and he went for his phone, we exchanged a brief and somber look.

I think we both realized what had happened: Jack had said he loved me, but I hadn't said it back.

CHAPTER
Nine

Being questioned at the Merryville Police Station wasn't as bad as I'd thought it would be. They left me to stew in a tiny, windowless room for about an hour, but I had a cup of mediocre coffee and a copy of the *Merryville Gazette* to keep me company. The entire front page of the paper was devoted to the cat show and Phillip's murder.

Ama had written a great series of interwoven stories, with sidebars about the history of the M-CFO, Phillip Denford's personal and professional life, and a brief guide to cat shows. She'd also gotten a great picture of the prize table before the collar dangle went missing. The dangle in its cage had caught the light from the flash and appeared as a spark of pure energy on the page. The picture was beautifully framed, at just the right angle to capture the lavish table setting. The only slight flaw to the picture was that it captured a person just in the foreground. The figure was too blurry to even tell if it was a man or a woman—just a pale blur of an arm, really—and I guessed that Ama had done her best to crop out the unwanted element from her otherwise postcard-perfect picture.

I read the articles carefully. They didn't tell me anything I didn't already know, but it was nice to have all the facts and factoids that were swimming around in my head laid out in clean, precise prose.

Eventually Sean—whom I'd insisted on calling before I left Jack's—arrived, and Gil Dixon came in to question me right on his heels. Jack had wanted to sit in, but both Sean and Gil nixed that plan.

"Ms. McHale, I've read through the statement you gave the day of the murder. Is there anything in that statement you would like to amend?"

Sean laid a restraining hand on my arm. He leaned in close. "Is everything in the statement true? A simple yes or no."

"Of course," I said, taken aback that he might think I'd lied.

Gil raised his eyebrows. "Let's face it: All of your words may have been true, but you did lie by omission when you left out the bit about Phillip Denford, our victim, being at your house within an hour of his death.

So don't get all prickly with me for asking whether you may have left out something else."

I sighed. "It's all true," I whispered.

"My client stands by the statement she gave the authorities," Sean said. Obviously I knew Sean was a lawyer, but I was still shocked at how formal he sounded responding to Gil. It was heartening to know I had him on my side.

"It is my understanding that you met with Phillip Denford on the morning of August eighteenth at your shop"—he shuffled some papers—"Trendy Tails, located at 801 Maple Avenue. Can you describe the nature of that meeting?"

I had opened my mouth to answer, but Sean beat me to it. "My client declines to answer that question."

"No, I don't," I said, shaking my head. "We were talking about business."

"What about business?" Gil asked.

"Izzy," Sean hissed.

"Mr. Denford said he was going to make knockoffs of my animal-apparel designs and he'd probably run me out of business. He was just giving me fair warning."

Sean face-palmed. He swiveled his head to look at me. "Why did you want me here if you weren't going to follow my advice?"

"Because you're my lawyer."

"But what good is having a lawyer if you don't listen to him?"

"I'm listening to you. I just disagreed about whether I should answer that question or not. I don't see the point in trying to keep it a secret. Someone Phillip worked with must have known what he was doing and that he was planning to talk to me. I mean, it's not like Phillip just phoned up a Korean textile manufacturer and sent them the sample of my cat's pajamas. He has an army of people to do that sort of thing. One of them would eventually come forward. Besides, I didn't do anything wrong, so I don't have anything to hide."

"You're killing me, Izzy."

It was the second time that evening that a man had said that to me. I was starting to feel insulted.

"Look," I said to Gil Dixon, "I don't have much to tell you. Phillip was in my shop until eight fifteen. Even if Phillip went to the ballroom straight from my house, there's no way Pris had time to kill him. She lives too far away."

Gil's smile was bemused. "But you know who lives a lot closer to the show venue? You. I've got statements from three people, including one Ruth Kimmey, whose table is right by yours, all saying you were late to the show. If you followed Phillip from Trendy Tails to the cat show, you could have killed him, gotten home to clean up, and made it back to the show by nine fifteen, which is when Ruth Kimmey said you arrived."

"Oh."

Sean closed his eyes and exhaled hard. "This is why you listen to your lawyer."

Honestly, I'd realized that Phillip's visit gave me motive for murder, but I hadn't realized how neatly my story fit the timeline of his death. Opportunity *and* motive, I thought. I was in deep doo-doo. I thought about mentioning that Wanda could verify that I was at Trendy Tails when she arrived, but she hadn't gotten to the store until almost nine that morning. That still gave me forty-five minutes to drive to the North Woods Hotel, kill Phillip, get home, and change—easy peasy given that my house was only about five minutes from the hotel. I'd given Pris an alibi, but now I sorely needed one of my own.

"Do you now or have you ever owned a pair of grooming shears or a set of pet-grooming tools?"

"Aha! No. I have not. Not ever. I've always taken Jinx and Packer to Pris's for grooming. I'm scared I'll cut one of them if I try to do it myself. Those shears are sharp."

"They are, indeed," Gil deadpanned.

"Izzy. Seriously. Be quiet," Sean pleaded.

I had needed to get Pris's alibi on the record because it was the right thing to do, but Sean was right that I didn't need to give the police any ammunition to use against me. I finally decided to follow my lawyer's advice.

While I was now squarely in the crosshairs of the investigation, the police had no basis to keep me. They'd arrested Pris the day of the murder because she was in possession of the stolen collar dangle. But there was no hard evidence linking either one of us to Phillip's murder.

Jack was waiting in the lobby when Sean and I emerged from the interrogation room. He jumped out of his chair when he saw us, but Sean waved him away.

"I think you've done enough for today. Don't you?" Sean snapped.

Jack actually looked guilty, but he leaned forward on his toes in a time-honored stance of male aggression. This had been a long, hard day for him, and I was worried he'd take out all his pent-up emotion on Sean. I held up my hands to quiet them both.

"Sean, that's not fair. Jack was doing his job. That doesn't mean he liked it. And everything is fine now."

"Fine? You call this fine?"

"Keep it down," Jack growled.

"Listen. I just want to go home," I said with a sigh of pure exhaustion.

"I'll drive you," Jack said. I'd left my car at his place and he'd driven me the few blocks over to the police station.

"No. I've got this." Sean ran his fingers through his sable hair, sending the loose curls pointing in a dozen directions.

"Oh, for the love of . . . Do we have to flip a coin?" I pulled Jack aside. "Let Sean give me a ride. I didn't do exactly as he told me to in the interview room, and I think he'd like to be able to do something concrete to help me. I'll see you tomorrow. Don't forget we're having dinner with Jolly and Rena tomorrow night."

Jack swept the room with a glare, as though he were willing all his colleagues—not to mention Sean— to disappear. Finally, he leaned down and planted an awkward peck on my forehead. "Fine. I'll see you tomorrow." I started to turn away, but he caught me by the arm. "Izzy, I need you to know that I'm sorry about this."

I offered him a weak smile. "Nothing to be sorry about. You wouldn't be my Jack if you didn't play by the rules. It'll all be okay."

The irony wasn't wasted on me: I was the one up to my eyeballs in trouble, but I'd spent the last five minutes trying to convince my two manly protectors not to worry.

Sean and I drove back to Trendy Tails in a silence that was broken the minute we walked through the front door. Rena, Aunt Dolly, my mom, and both my sisters, Lucy and Dru, were waiting inside, and they pummeled me with questions as soon as I appeared.

"Good heavens, Izzy," my mother said. "What have you gotten yourself into?"

"And what can we do to get you out of it?" Aunt Dolly asked.

I filled them in on my discussion with Phillip and talked them through how it alibied Pris but left me in the lurch.

"I'm so sorry I didn't tell you about Phillip's threat right away," I said to Rena.

"No, it's for the best that you kept quiet. If you'd told me, I really would have killed him. And then where would we be?"

"Trying to figure out how to get you off the hook instead of me."

"There's no *trying* about it," Rena said with a decisive swish of her hand. "I was here with you when Phillip came to call. And I stayed with you until we left for the cat show. Tell them that."

I grabbed my friend and gave her a big hug. "Thanks for that. But I already talked to the police and didn't mention being with anyone that morning. If I suddenly say, 'Gee, I forgot to tell you that my best friend was with me all morning and can corroborate my story,' it's going to look pretty hinky. Besides, if people at the cat show noticed I was late, I'd lay good money they noticed you were on time."

"Besides," Sean said. "I'm standing right here. As an officer of the court, I can't allow you guys to perjure yourselves. I appreciate the sentiment, but truth and a healthy dose of silence are Izzy's best allies here."

"Actually," Dolly piped up, "I really can give you that alibi."

"Dolly, you weren't here," I said with a sigh.

"Not here, here. But I, uh, might have been next door."

"Dorothy!" my mother gasped.

"Don't judge me, Edie. I've been a widow for a very long time."

It seemed to take a moment for the penny to drop for the rest of us. Dru blushed crimson, Rena and Lucy busted out laughing and high-fived each other, and Sean and I just stared in wonder.

"You spent the night with Richard Greene?" I finally asked.

"Young lady, don't look a gift horse in the mouth. You're lucky I was there."

"What exactly did you see?" Sean asked.

"Oh God, no," Lucy moaned. "Don't describe it." Lucy had always been the sister with the naughty streak, the one who sneaked out of the house in the middle of the night and hung out with boys who were too old for her. Normally, I found her irreverence amusing, but at that moment I wanted to clap my hand over her mouth.

"Lucy, that's entirely inappropriate, especially in mixed company." My sister Dru could be a stick-in-the-mud on occasion, but she was saying what everyone in the room was thinking.

"Seriously, Dolly. What did you see that morning?" Sean asked again.

"Richard was in the kitchen making coffee when I heard a car pull up outside. A man got out. It must have been Phillip Denford, but I didn't have my eyes in yet." My aunt had worn contacts for decades. "The car pulled away and then, maybe ten minutes later, I heard a honk outside and I looked out to see the man getting back in the car."

Sean's eyes bored into my poor aunt. His interrogation was tougher than anything Gil Dixon had handed me. "What else? Did you see anything else?"

"Not until a little after nine, when I heard Wanda's old rust bucket pull up. That car grinds and rattles more than my left hip. I looked outside again and saw Izzy dashing to her own car with Jinx's cage in one hand and a stack of critter clothes in the other."

Dru sighed. "That doesn't help at all. Unless you were staring out the window the whole time, Izzy could have left and come back with you being none the wiser."

"I don't suppose you were just standing there watching the street—were you, Aunt Dolly?" Lucy asked with a sly smile.

For the first time in my life, I watched my aunt Dolly blush. "No. I wasn't just standing there. I might have been a little preoccupied. You're right. I guess as alibis go, the one I'm offering is pretty weak."

"But this is a great help," Sean said. "Are you sure the car left after Phillip got out?"

I saw where he was going. I slapped my own forehead. "I totally forgot about hearing the car honk right before Phillip left."

"I'm sure of what I saw. And what I heard," Dolly said adamantly.

"This is huge," Sean said.

He was right. I didn't have an alibi, but Dolly's story made one thing abundantly clear. The morning that Phillip Denford had visited Trendy Tails, the morning he was murdered, he was not alone.

Eventually my mother called a halt to the evening. It was late, and I'd had a hard day, she said. I needed to sleep.

She was absolutely correct, but I still asked Rena to hang back. I finally had to tell her all about Phillip's threat to ruin our business. While she'd picked up bits and pieces from our conversation about my brush with the police, she needed to know every detail.

When I finished recounting our desperate plight, Rena threw her arms around me and gave me a huge hug. For someone her size, Rena was surprisingly strong, and her most heartfelt hugs could be painful. This one hurt.

"I'm so sorry," she said.

"You have no reason to be sorry. If either of us

should be apologizing, it should be me. I dragged you into this business in the first place."

"You didn't exactly twist my arm. Besides, I don't know about you, but I don't plan to back down yet. No sense closing up shop because we may have a little competition."

We sat across from each other at the red table, each lost in thought.

"I've been in a few fights in my day," Rena said, "and I'm always hopelessly outmatched. I mean, most sixth graders outweigh me. But I use what should be a disadvantage to help me conquer my foe. I'm light, so I'm fast. I'm short, so it's easier for me to duck from blows. . . . My body just isn't at the height most people naturally hit at. I use what I have. And I'm not saying I've never taken a beating, but I do pretty well."

I smiled. "And this relates to our situation how?"

"We have to play to our strengths. Phillip said we wouldn't be able to compete because you make so much of our product by hand. So we turn that into a selling point. Our stuff is handmade, not made in a factory. There are lots of people who will pay extra money to have something sewn or crocheted or knitted by hand."

I nodded. "I like that. Using our apparent weakness as a marketing tool. We can also play up the fact that we can hand-tailor our garments. Phillip's mass manufacturing works only if they make tons of outfits in a few uniform sizes. We can take measurements of actual pets, assuring a better fit."

"And we can customize goods easily, by adding embroidered names or using specific colors and fabrics."

Rena leaned across the table to high-five me. "His company can do more, but we can do better . . . no matter how good the quality of his knockoffs."

I leaned back in my chair, thinking about our plan to distinguish ourselves as the source for custom canine and kitty clothes. I liked it. We were going couture.

"You know," Rena said hesitantly, "another way we could separate ourselves from Phillip's market would be to provide pets and their humans with matching clothes."

Her suggestion knocked the breath out of me. When Casey and I had moved to Madison to attend college, I'd studied fashion design. When he was done with his residency in Merryville, we were supposed to move to the Big Apple together so I could pursue a career as a women's-wear designer. When I got left behind in Merryville, I started selling pet clothes because I'd had some luck selling them in Ingrid's Gift Haus and because Merryville didn't seem like a place people would trust for handmade dresses. But in some little corner of my heart, that dream had lived on.

I don't know why I never thought of combining the two pursuits into a single business, but it seemed like pure genius.

"Do you think we could do it? Do you think people would buy?"

Rena grinned. "Are you kidding? Some people might stick to clothing for their pets, but if you dress your pets regularly, there has to be some occasion on which you'd want to coordinate, right? Little mini bridesmaid dresses, for example. Or clothes for some pet-related event, like a cat show or a local festival." Rena shrugged. "It might end up being a fairly small part of the business, but it would definitely catch people's attention."

I laughed out loud. It felt like a giant weight had been lifted. The suggested changes might not save us, but they gave me hope. And at that minute, hope seemed like a valuable commodity.

Rena rested her arms on the table and looked serious. "Biggest obstacle I see is the name of the store."

"What's wrong with Trendy Tails? It's been working for us all this time."

"Right. For selling pet clothes. But if we add human clothes to the mix . . . What fashionable woman is going to want to wear a 'Trendy Tails Original'? It's just too petlike."

"Can we afford to change the brand so late in the game? I don't want us to lose our existing customers."

"No. It's easy. We have addresses for just about every customer we've had in here. At least an e-mail address. So we send out a postcard and e-mail blast to let them know about the change. Then you keep the Trendy Tails Web domain name and have it automatically redirect to the site for the new store."

"I understood about half of that, but it all sounds good. So what can we name the store that encompasses humans and pets?"

Rena closed one eye and leaned back, as though she were preparing to ward off a blow. "I was thinking maybe 'Swag and Wags'?"

"I love it. And I love you for sticking beside me through all this."

Rena smiled. "Where else would I be?"

CHAPTER
Ten

I was awakened the following morning by someone pounding on the front door of Trendy Tails loud enough to rouse me from my hibernation on the third floor.

I yanked on my robe and scampered down the stairs as fast as my half-asleep brain could propel me. If the knocking was loud enough to wake me, it was loud enough to wake Ingrid and Harvey, and it was certainly loud enough to wake my neighbor Richard. Even though we'd reached a state of détente, thanks to his relationship with my aunt Dolly, I didn't want to poke the bear.

Indeed, when I hit the second landing, Ingrid stuck her head out of her door. "Is someone dead?"

"I don't know. I don't think so."

"Well, that's a righteous commotion someone's making. Someone had better be dead."

The banging began again in earnest. "I'll let you know what's up," I promised Ingrid before starting down the stairs again.

"Coming, coming, coming," I muttered as I flew down the last flight.

I was surprised to see Marigold Aames at my front door.

Knowing she'd dated Jack in the past, I was particularly self-conscious of my bedhead and robe.

"Good morning, Mari," I said as I ushered her inside. In deference to the hot August day, she was wearing a cute green sundress, and she gave her arms a vigorous rub as she walked into the air-conditioned coolness of Trendy Tails. "What's going on?" I asked.

As soon as the words were out of my mouth, I realized they weren't entirely polite. But then I decided that I didn't entirely care.

"I'm actually looking for Jack."

I tried to scoop my jaw off the floor and reaffix it to my face. "Jack? Seriously? You came here to find Jack?"

"Well, yeah."

"He's not here."

"Oh. Okay. I thought you two . . ." She was playing with her necklace, and she looked about ready to jump out of her skin.

"We are. But he's not here. And even if he were, it would be a little weird for you to come looking for him here."

She squinted and shook her head, like I was talking gibberish.

"I didn't mean any offense. I just really need to find Jack, and I don't know where he lives. I don't even have his cell number. But I knew where to find you."

"If you wait down here, I'll run upstairs and give him a call."

"Or you could just give me his number. I don't want to take up more of your time."

I paused. Part of me thought, Heck, this was none of my business. Give her the number and let her and Jack do whatever they wanted together. The other part of me, the part that sounded like Rena and my sister Lucy, said no way. Whatever this woman was up to with Jack, she'd have to go through me to get it done.

"I'll be right back," I said.

I dashed up the stairs to call Jack and then threw on some clothes. I thought about the girlie dress Mari was wearing and took a few extra minutes to put up my hair and swipe some gloss across my lips.

I managed to make it back downstairs and start a pot of coffee before Jack arrived.

"Cream? Sugar?" I offered her.

"No, thanks. Peter, Phillip, and I all take our coffee

black. The only one who likes the fancy drinks is Marsha."

That seemed like very detailed information for an assistant to know, not just about her boss but about his family.

"You four travel together a lot."

Mari waved her hand. "We did. All the time. Phillip always had some sort of business engagement, and he traveled throughout the Midwest."

"But why would Marsha come with him?"

"Nothing better to do, she said. May as well see some of America rather than rattle around in their massive house all alone."

"But what about Peter? As an artist, he surely had reason to stay at home in . . ."

"Duluth," Mari supplied. "Peter's a mess," she volunteered. "He'd be an artist if he had access to raw materials, but he needs heavy equipment and expensive metal to do his art, so he just doesn't do it."

"Still, why follow his dad around?"

Mari shrugged. "I think he does it more for Marsha's company than Phillip's. Sure, he's always trying to get his dad to foot the bill for something, but Phillip almost always says no."

"But Marsha and Peter are close?"

"Oh yes. When Peter's mother died, his father sent him off to boarding school. When he arrived home after graduation, he was at loose ends. Phillip would only pay for college if Peter agreed to major in business or economics, so Peter just stayed home. By that point, Phillip had married Marsha, and she was less than a decade older than Peter. I guess they bonded over Phillip's neglect. As near as I can tell, they're each the best friend the other has."

What a sad, strange family, I thought. I was going to press Mari for more of the skinny on the Denfords, but Jack was bounding up my porch stairs.

When he walked in the door, Mari flew into his arms. "Oh, Jack. I'm so glad you're here."

Jack met my gaze over Mari's head. He raised his eyebrows in question and I shrugged an answer.

"What do you need?" Jack started to pull away from Marigold's embrace, but she clung to him like a limpet.

"I've just been beside myself since Phillip died," she said. "He was such a good mentor for me. I don't know what I'll do without him." Her voice was rising into near hysterics.

"Hush, now, Goldilocks. It's going to be okay. What did you need to tell me?"

Jack firmly pushed Mari away from him, and she raised her hands to wipe the tears from her cheeks. She'd left mascara smudges on his clean white T-shirt. I felt a flare of jealousy, like she'd marked my property.

"I'm sorry. This has just been such an emotional whirlwind, trying to keep the show on track as I know Phillip would have wanted, when all I want to do is grieve." She shook herself and scrubbed at her face.

"I know this must be hard for you," Jack said. "You worked closely with Phillip, and death is always difficult."

"But I needed to tell you something," Mari said. "I feel so guilty about not mentioning it to the officer who took my statement. I mean, what if I'm helping someone get away with murder? Last night I barely slept, so I had to tell you this morning first thing."

"Tell me what?" Jack sounded like he was losing patience.

"It's about Phillip. He and Marsha were having problems."

"How do you know that?" Jack asked.

"Peter told me. He said he'd taken his dad to see a divorce lawyer."

"I'll have to ask Peter about that."

"Of course," she snuffled. "But there's more. Phillip and Marsha had a prenup. If they got a divorce, Marsha would have been penniless."

"Did Peter tell you about that, too?" I asked.

Mari tilted her head to look at me, as though she'd forgotten I was even in the room. "No. Phillip told me about the prenup one evening when we were, you know, having a few drinks after a long day. He got a little tipsy, and he just blurted it out. He was very clear, though, that she would get nothing."

Mari paused for dramatic effect. "I think Marsha may have killed Phillip," she said in a stage whisper.

"It sounds like she might have had motive, but we're going to need more to go on than that," Jack said.

She batted him playfully on the arm. "I know that. That's why you're the police and I'm not. I just thought you should have full information. It's not like Marsha's going to offer up her motive when you talk to her."

"Well, I appreciate the help."

"Yes. Well. I guess I should get going."

"I do need to get cleaned up for work," Jack said. "I was so worried when Izzy called that I rushed out without a proper shirt and tie."

"This look always suited you. We still on for coffee tomorrow?"

Jack looked at me, then down at tiny little Mari. "Yeah. Sure. I'll pick you up at ten."

She fluttered her fingers at Jack and then gave me a less flirtatious wave. "Thanks for being such a sport, Izzy."

As soon as the door closed behind her, I spun on Jack. "A sport? What was that supposed to mean? And coffee? You're going to get coffee with her?"

"Yes. She's an old friend. It's the polite thing to do."

He reached out to take my arm and pull me close. "Are you maybe a little jealous? I think I like that."

"Oh, honestly. I'm not jealous."

"You sure? Not even a little bit?"

My eyes fixed on the mascara stain on his T-shirt, and my heart plummeted. "I am. I'm being one of 'those' women."

He laughed. "What women?"

"The kind that cling to their boyfriends and get upset when they even talk to another woman. I don't want to be that kind of girl."

Jack leaned in and gently brushed his lips across mine. "I think you're entitled to a bit of jealousy. After what happened with Casey I can imagine you're a little low on trust."

"Maybe. But still, I'm a grown woman."

"Believe me, baby, I know that," he growled. Then he got serious. "I understand why you're jealous. Mari is a flirt. That's one of the things I liked about her. *Fifteen years ago.* But look in my eyes."

I tilted up my chin to meet eyes the color of the heart of a flame. "You have no reason to be jealous. I'm in this for real. And there's a reason I broke up with Mari. I realized that I wanted someone simple and honest rather than someone who plays games. I wanted someone just like you."

Warmth radiated from my chest to my limbs, and

I had to resist the urge to jump into his arms. We both had work and no time for nooky. Instead I stepped back and smoothed down my Trendy Tails golf shirt.

"What do you think of her claims about Marsha?"

He shrugged. "I don't know. Obviously, we're checking every angle, and that bit of information may come in handy. Or not. Lots of people talk to divorce attorneys and then quickly change their minds."

Jack may not have been swayed by Mari's little tidbit, but I knew how I'd be spending the day: trying to get the dirt on Marsha Denford.

As promised, I tromped up the steps to reassure Ingrid that everything was fine.

"No one's dead. Except Phillip, of course, but that's old news."

Ingrid ducked her head back into her apartment to look around.

"Do you mind if we go up to your place for a few minutes? I know you need to get to the show, but there's something I've been meaning to talk to you about."

"Of course!"

Ingrid followed me up to the third-floor apartment. She made herself at home on my worn sofa. I liked to think of it as shabby chic, but it was really just shabby. I popped into the galley kitchen to get us a couple squares of Rena's coffee cake and a couple mugs of coffee.

By the time I brought out the morning goodies, Ingrid had been mobbed by my creatures. Jinx had claimed her lap, and the giant cat took up every inch, while Packer had found a way to lie next to Ingrid's leg so that every part of the dog was touching a part of Ingrid.

"Thank you, dear," she said as she took the coffee, and I set the cake on the side table next to her elbow.

"Is everything okay?" I asked. Ingrid was a straight shooter. She was being uncharacteristically hesitant about speaking her mind.

"Actually, no." She took a deep breath. "It's Harvey. Last winter he had a clot in his leg. Now he just had some tests done and they've found two more."

"Oh, Ingrid. I'm so sorry. Will he be all right?"

Ingrid set her jaw. "I don't honestly know. What I do know is that he needs good medical treatment. So we're heading back to Boca next week. The doctor gave him some compression socks to wear on the plane, and once we get there, he'll have close access to really good hospitals and doctors. Plus, he'll be closer to his daughter and the grandkids."

"That makes sense. We'll all be sad to see you go, but I don't blame you for wanting to get Harvey the treatment he needs."

"Well, here's the thing. Harvey's not going to get any better. The best they can do is keep things from getting worse. He's not going to be able to fly anymore, and I just don't know when—if—I'm going to make it back to Merryville."

If? Was there really a possibility that Ingrid would never come home?

"You could fly back for a long weekend now and then, right? Even if Harvey can't?"

"Oh, honey, I wish it were that simple. Getting old's a bitch." She stroked Jinx's head and listened to her purr motor up. "I've had a couple of tests, too, and the doctor saw a spot on my lung."

"A spot."

"As in cancer." As if to prove her point, she began to cough, scaring Jinx away and setting Packer to whining.

"But you've never smoked a day in your life," I said when her coughing fit subsided.

"Me, no. But Arnold smoked like a chimney. Do you know how many evenings we spent sitting in that front parlor, reading and watching *I Love Lucy* while Arnold sucked down a whole pack of Lucky Strikes?"

"That isn't fair."

"Life rarely is, my dear. Now, I may just beat this cancer thing, but with both of us sick, we have to face facts that our snowbird plan just isn't going to work. So I want you to have the house."

"What?"

"The house. I'm signing the deed over to you to-morrow. I'll need a dollar or something to make it a legal transaction. I don't know. The lawyer's got it all figured out so you don't have to pay much but the government won't treat it as a gift. If it's more money than you have on hand, we'll consider it a loan."

"What am I going to do with this big ol' house?"

Ingrid threw back her head and laughed. "Just what you're doing with it now. Run your business here, live here, rent out one of the floors. Maybe to that Wanda child."

"Wanda's only seventeen. She still lives with her parents."

Ingrid harrumphed. "Mark my words—that one will need a home sometime soon. Hetty Tucker says the girl's been running around with Will Thomas, the preacher's son from Christ the King out on Highway 59. She's gonna be knocked up in two shakes of a lamb's tail."

"Ingrid Nyquist, there's no way you can know such a thing," I chided.

"I think we've established that I'm an old lady. I've seen lots of young girls in my day, and I'm pretty good at spotting the ones who get talked right out of their good sense and their panties."

I laughed. We both did. And then I sobered, thinking I might not get many more times like this.

"Look, Izzy, I never had children of my own, but you've come mighty close over the years. I want you to have this house. Even if you just turn around and sell it, I'll know that it brought you some joy. Some value. Now, let me have my way."

"Yes, ma'am."

CHAPTER
Eleven

On the second full day of the cat show, all of the attention turned to the ballroom and the conformation competitions, where the cats would be judged against the standards for each breed: Were their ears set at the proper angle? Were their bodies the correct shape? Did their profiles match some ideal (if arbitrary) standard? Each of the judging rings was packed with onlookers, and you could tell when every round ended by the squeaks and gasps and moans of the audience.

Rena and I set up our booth, and I agreed to man it while Rena took a tour of the floor to pass out cards and, of course, get a look-see at all the action.

"Are you the designer?"

I looked up to find Peter Denford standing at the corner of our table, that familiar Joe Time Coffee cup in his hand. I'd seen him hanging around the show and had even seen him the morning of his father's death, but we'd yet to actually speak.

"Yes. Izzy McHale," I offered, extending my hand.

He shook my hand, and I couldn't help but notice the calluses on his fingers. He might play the part of artistic dilettante, but he actually worked hard at something.

"I'm glad to get to meet you," I said. "The collar ornament you designed is beautiful. I loved the open-work surrounding the gems."

He waved off my compliment. "As my father said, the drawing's the easy part."

His dad had said that? Still more evidence that Phillip was a complete sleazeball.

"I enjoyed the design work, but my real passion is for sculpture. Large-scale metalwork, actually. The exact opposite of that little charm I drew. I rarely find the patience to work on smaller projects like jewelry. I mean, there's a reason my father didn't have me execute my own drawing. The jeweler is the real hero."

"Jolly's a good friend. I'll let her know."

"I like your work," he said.

"Oh, uh, thanks. Do you own pets?" I asked.

He grinned, and there was something charming about his smile. He had deep lines running from his nose to the corners of his lips, and when he smiled, those lines nearly bracketed his whole mouth.

"No. No pets. I leave the animals to my father. I just like your designs. Hipster designs for hipster pets. I like the social commentary."

"Thank you."

I didn't intend my parkas and pj's to be social commentary, but if this artist chose to view my work that way, I wasn't going to stop him. If I told him that I designed the clothes just because I thought the animals looked cute in them, he'd probably think I was a loon, so I chose to take his comment as a compliment.

"I'm sorry for your loss," I added, suddenly realizing that this was the very *first* thing I should have said to the man.

He looked at me quizzically before the light of recognition dawned in his eyes. "Oh, of course. I keep forgetting. Thank you."

I just stared at him, taken aback by how nonchalant he seemed to be about his father's death.

He must have picked up on my shock—and possibly the undercurrent of judgment—in my eyes, because he ducked his head and let forth a self-deprecating chuckle. "I know I sound like a horrible son. It's just that my father and I weren't that close."

"I'm sorry to hear that." My own poor father, living in a house full of gregarious women, hardly said boo and kept himself holed up in his study with mountains of history books to read. But if he were gone, I'd miss him like crazy. I felt bad for Peter that he didn't have that kind of bond with his father.

He shrugged. "My father had his own interests and, uh, pursuits, and I had mine."

"Like your art."

"Precisely. My father didn't think my artwork was a serious career. It was a hobby, he said, like his cat shows. The difference was he'd earned a time-consuming and expensive hobby by being a crackerjack businessman. I had earned nothing."

"But at least he came to you when he needed the collar ornament designed."

Peter laughed. "Actually, he didn't. I'd heard about his plans from . . . dinner, and I took it upon myself to draw the design. He didn't even pay me for it. Or ask me to execute it."

"Wow. That must have burned."

"No. It's just the way our relationship was. Trust me. I'm a grown man, and I've learned to be self-sufficient over the years. I can take care of myself without my daddy pitching in."

From across the aisle, Ruth Kimmey gave me a little wave and I returned it. Peter watched our exchange with a half smile on his face.

"I see you've made Ruth's acquaintance."

"Yes. She's been very helpful, showing me around."

He took a sip of his coffee. "I'm sure she has. She's

probably told you about the good old days when these shows were a little wilder."

I blushed.

"Mmm-hmmm. Did she tell you that she and my father had a fling? It was between my mom and Marsha, so my father wasn't technically cheating. But something tells me it wasn't a coincidence that Ruth's big Russian blue, Jampaws Mr. Jumbo, took home the crown that year."

"Ruth?"

He laughed. "She didn't always look like that. I remember her from back then. I've always had a thing for older women, and I had a big ol' crush on her then."

I had actually been thinking that she didn't seem like the type to dally, but I couldn't help but turn to study Ruth through the lens of that bit of information. I could see it: the gray hair a rich auburn brown, those fine cheekbones, her delicate build, less grannylike glasses on her face.

"Huh."

"The march of time, right?"

"I guess."

"So, Izzy, I wanted to make a suggestion to you, one struggling artist to another. I assume you have a Web storefront?"

"Sure. We do good volume over the Internet. Merryville's a tourist town, and I get a surprising number of regulars from the community, but most of our sales are online."

"Have you heard of theartisanway.com?" He took another sip of his coffee before setting it on the edge of our display table.

"No. Should I have?"

He grinned. "Maybe not yet. We're a start-up right now, just getting off the ground. But we can make you a lot of money if you give us a shot."

I sighed. *We.* The father was trying to kill my business and the son was trying to save it. I wondered if Peter knew about his father's plans to take over my niche in the marketplace.

"See, the great thing about theartisanway.com is that it's strictly high-end handcrafted goods, but it's not limited to pet stuff. So a shopper may come to the site looking for a gift for his dad, find Trendy Tails, and end up buying Dad a sweater for his dachshund. Or the shopper may come looking for a trench coat for herself and find one for her beagle on the Trendy Tails page. It's a way to reach a whole market that didn't even know they needed your products."

"So it's like an online craft fair."

"For hipsters," he agreed with a nod. "And rich people. Basically, your clientele."

I had plenty of average Joes who bought ruffs for their cats and little fleece booties for their pups, but he was right that I needed to appeal to that group of buyers if I wanted Trendy Tails—soon to be Swag and Wags—to grow.

"It's perfect for you. We'll accept only handmade items, so anything made in a factory—no matter how high-quality—can't be sold on the site." Again, I wondered if he knew about his father's efforts to undercut my business, whether that was the very reason he was approaching me. Was he hoping to nurture my business so it would be a legitimate competitor with his dead father's business? Or was he genuinely interested in growing small businesses?

"Well, you've given me a lot to think about. How much does it cost to participate?"

He held still, gauging my reaction. "Right now, a thousand a month plus two percent of your pretax net sales. We're upping to four percent of initial sales after the first one hundred accounts."

I let out a low whistle. With my margins, that would mean a serious hit.

Peter jumped right back in to assuage my fears. "That thousand, though, that provides all your technical support. We're negotiating to hire a full-time Web designer who would help artists set up their stores, organize products so they're easier to find, basically do everything other than taking pictures of your stuff. He'll even pump up your copy for you. And our clients are quality seekers. They're willing to pay more than your in-store customers. You can make up that two percent with slight markups to your prices that won't impact demand."

On its face, the prospect was compelling. Rena and I had just talked about emphasizing the handmade custom quality of our work, and theartisanway.com would be drawing people who were interested in supporting that kind of business. But in the end, I had no idea how Web marketing worked. Maybe this was the opportunity of a lifetime. Or maybe it was a lot of hocus-pocus. Either way, I couldn't make a move without input from my business partner, Rena.

"You keep saying 'we' when you talk about this program. Who else is involved?"

"I have a silent partner, who prefers to remain silent."

"It's not your father?"

He laughed. "Not exactly. Why?"

"I am a little persnickety about whom I do business with."

"Well, he's gone anyway."

He had a point, but I was still leery of getting involved in anything to do with Phillip Denford, his kith, or his kin.

"Listen," Peter said, "some of us are going to lunch tomorrow at Red, White and Bleu. Basically, me and all the people running the cat show. Why don't you come with us?"

"I have to check with Rena, make sure she doesn't mind covering the booth and getting a doggy bag, but if she's okay with it, I'd love to tag along."

Maybe, I thought, *I'll find a new way to make a little cash. And maybe I'll learn a little more about a murderer.*

Rena had asked me and Jack to join her and Jolly Nielson for dinner that evening. Though Rena was playing hostess, we were dining on the main floor at Trendy Tails. Rena shared a place with her unpredictable father, and Jolly lived out of a corner of her studio. The old dining room at 801 Maple had become the official gathering spot for our circle of friends, and since Rena knew her way around that kitchen as well as she did her own, it made sense for us to meet in the store.

Still, while we were eating on what amounted to my own turf, the evening belonged to Rena and Jolly.

Even though Rena and I had been best friends since we were in kindergarten—even before Sean Tucker moved to town and rounded out the Musketeers—she hadn't come out to me until just a year before. Even then, she rarely talked about her love life.

That is, until she and Jolly started dating. Jolly had eight years on us, and she was comfortable in her own skin. With midnight hair, soft amber eyes, and a gently curvy body that she clothed in long dresses and her own nature-inspired jewelry, Jolly defined "earth mother."

She and Rena were peanut butter and chocolate: starkly different but oh so good together.

Jack and I regularly went on double dates with Rena and Jolly, so there was nothing unusual about Rena inviting us to dine with them, but I could tell that the evening was special somehow. If nothing else, Rena was wearing a dress, and when I asked what the occasion was, she actually blushed.

As usual, I didn't bring much to the table other than a couple bottles of chardonnay. I was an adequate cook, but I was surrounded by greatness. Jolly, who had a knack for putting together a good cheese board, had laid out brie, fig preserves, sliced fresh stone fruit, a sharp manchego, and some delicate sesame crackers. We sat around the cherry-red table, sipping wine and munching on cheese while Rena put the finishing touches on her famous portobello tacos. Along with a simply dressed salad of mixed greens, baby beets, and goat cheese from a farmer one county over, they would be dinner. And Jack had brought dessert: a mascarpone-and-raspberry tart with a crisp chocolate crust.

Seriously, with the three of them in my life, it was a miracle I wasn't as big as a house.

Jack spread a cracker with fig and brie, then topped it with a slice of plum and held it to my lips. While he wasn't usually all that affectionate in public, Jolly and Rena didn't count as public.

As he leaned in to kiss a crumb from the corner of my lips, Val—Rena's chocolate roan ferret—popped her head up above the edge of the table. She'd scrambled into Rena's vacant seat and was eyeing the spread with eager eyes. Before she could decide which of the many tasty tidbits she should try to snatch, Jolly whisked her up into her arms.

"Bad girl, Val. I thought we were teaching you table manners."

Val wriggled out of Jolly's arms, took a flying leap onto a pile of kitty capelets, and then slithered herself away to frolic in the front of the store.

Rena bumped open the kitchen door with her behind and carried in the tacos in one hand and the salad in the other, all the while trying not to trip over Jinx, who was doing figure eights around her legs. She set the dishes on the table and we started passing them around.

"So, uh, Jolly and I have some news," Rena said, her plate piled with food she had yet to touch.

She reached out her hand, and Jolly brought hers up to nestle inside it. For a few seconds, they simply stared at each other, loopy smiles on their faces.

Jolly giggled for no apparent reason, then cleared her throat. "We're getting married."

I nearly choked on a piece of beet. "What?"

"We're getting married," Rena repeated, the grin on her face growing wider.

"That's great news," Jack said, pushing back from the table and walking around to give them both big bear hugs. I leapt to my feet and followed suit.

"I'm so happy for you two! When did you decide to get hitched? When's the wedding? Tell me everything," I insisted.

Rena laughed. "There's not that much to tell. We'd sort of been dancing around the idea for a few weeks, but then I finally decided to just ask. Scariest five minutes of my life before she said yes."

Jolly gave her a playful punch in the arm. "It was no more than two minutes, and you knew I'd say yes. I wasn't very subtle when I showed you a design for wedding bands."

"I was still nervous."

"So when are you going to do it? What are the plans?"

"There are still a lot of decisions to make, but we'd like to get married in October. We were thinking of a destination wedding. Renting a couple of cabins on the north shore of Lake Superior for a few close friends and family and getting married on the beach with a bonfire."

I sighed. "That sounds so romantic."

"Way to set the bar, ladies," Jack said.

I caught his eye, and we both blushed.

"Do you want to see the design for the rings?" Jolly asked. She was already out of her chair and rummaging in her purse.

"Dang it."

"Is the drawing missing?" Rena asked.

"Yes. I swear it was here."

Rena sighed. She got up from the table and walked over to the big oak armoire in the front room of the store, dragging her chair behind her.

"Val?" I asked.

"I imagine so." When we'd first opened Trendy Tails, Rena had brought Val with her all the time. Packer got along fine with the ferret, and other than a mutual raising of hackles when they both wanted to sleep on top of the armoire, Jinx and Val basically ignored each other. But like many ferrets, Val was a tiny thief. Eventually, she stole one too many wallets from our customers, and Rena started leaving her at home during the days. In the evenings, though, she brought Val so the beastie wouldn't get lonely.

Rena climbed on top of the chair to reach the top of the armoire and felt around up there for a few seconds. While she was searching the top of the cabinet, Val herself leapt onto the chair Rena stood on and climbed Rena like a tree. She sat on top of the armoire, looking offended, while Rena looted the space.

Rena returned to the table with a handful of goodies she'd found: a scrap of paper, a fountain pen, and a round gold locket without a chain.

"There it is," Jolly said, taking the scrap of paper from the pile.

She handed it to me. On it she'd sketched a beautiful ring: two vines loosely entwined topped by a single rose blossom that held a gem at its heart.

"Oh, Jolly. It's gorgeous."

She blushed. "Thank you. It's us, the two vines. Wrapped around each other but with space between us, and the rose is our love. Beautiful but, like all things in this world, fragile."

As she explained her work, she gently stroked the back of Rena's head. Rena reached up a hand so they rested their clasped fingers on Rena's shoulder. My heart melted for my dear friend.

"What else did you find?" I asked.

"The fountain pen looks like something Richard Greene would own. I'll walk it over to him in the morning, see if it's his. The locket, I have no idea."

Jolly reached down to take the locket from the table. She *tsk*ed softly. "See, that's just sloppy work," she said. "The jump ring that held the locket to a chain is bent. That's why I like to fuse everything."

"What do you mean?" I asked.

"Well, like that collar dangle I crafted for Phillip Denford. I hung it by a jump ring from the top of the wire cage. But instead of just bending the jump ring into place, I soldered it. Once it was awarded to the winner, I would have had to snip the ring apart so the dangle could be removed for evaluation by the gemologist, but in the meantime—while it was hanging on that table where people and animals were jostling it—it would stay in place instead of knocking against wires and possibly marring the finish on the platinum."

Rena smiled up at her. "You're so talented."

"Oh, shush. I'm just careful with precious things."

Okay, as happy as I was for the two of them, the goo-goo eyes and sweet nothings were getting to be a bit much. I took the locket from Rena's hand.

The outside of the locket was etched with the profile of a cat. I popped open its catch. Inside, there was no picture, just an engraving. *G.A. from P.D. Always.*

I closed the locket and handed it to Jack. "Does that look familiar to you?"

He turned it over in his hand. "No. Should it?"

"I swear I saw Pamela Rawlins wearing a locket just like this."

"But her initials are P.R."

"Exactly. And she hasn't been in the shop since the cat show started. So who does this one belong to?"

CHAPTER
Twelve

After dinner, the four of us lolled at the table, nibbling on Jack's luscious tart. If I hadn't been stuffed from all the food that came before, I would have wolfed down half the dessert. As it was, I was already thinking ahead to how delicious the tart would be for breakfast the next morning.

"So. About that locket," Jolly said. "I confess I'm intrigued."

"Well, I checked the armoire the last time Val was here, the day before we started setting up for the cat show, so it has to belong to someone who visited recently. Very recently."

I sighed. "We've hardly been here. If anyone would know who came in, it would be Wanda."

"Really?" Rena remarked. "You think Wanda would know?"

"No, not really."

The bottom line was that Wanda was a lovely girl who was generally on time. I trusted her to be polite to the customers and to call 911 if anything caught on fire. But she was seventeen. Trendy Tails was just a job for her, and a low-paying job at that. Even when we had customers, she spent as much time on her phone as actually helping them. And she was none too bright. She'd friended me on social media, but posted all the time about the smelly dogs and sheddy cats at "TT." Like I needed a code breaker to know what she was talking about.

Ingrid might have been right that Wanda was on track to be a teen mom, but I hoped she dodged that bullet. Poor child could barely keep her own life together. I couldn't imagine her being able to care for a child. And if she moved into the house? I'd never be able to hire more competent help.

In any event, the odds that Wanda could remember who had come into the store over the past few days were slim to none.

"Well," Jolly said, "it's probably someone related to the cat show. Maybe those lockets are some sort of Midwestern Cat Fanciers' Organization baubles. The equivalent of the gold watches that corporations used to give to long-serving employees."

"No. They were more personal than that. Inscribed. But I think you're right that it must be someone who is involved with the M-CFO. Otherwise, Pamela Rawlins having a similar necklace is just too coincidental."

I tapped the tines of my fork on my plate. "G.A. Who could that be? I've met a Sharon Andrews, a Donna Avilar, and a Toni Ackerson. All A's but no G's."

"And why would anyone from the cat show come to the store when they could do their shopping right there in the middle of the ballroom? It doesn't make sense."

"Well, the one person from the show who has definitely been here, other than Phillip Denford, of course, is Marigold Aames."

"But she would be M.A., not G.A.," Rena said around a mouthful of tart. Jolly frowned at her, and Rena grinned, showing off teeth covered in cookie crumbs. "Oh, come on. You don't love me for my table manners."

"G, G, G," I muttered. "Wait, Jack! When Mari Aames was here, you called her Goldilocks."

"Oh right," he said. "Old bad habit. When she was in high school, everyone called her Goldilocks, back when she had a bad perm and braces. She hated the nickname, but I picked it up from her high school friends who also attended UMD. She spent so much time trying to retrain us all to call her Mari."

"See," I said, "that's even more intimate. Not only is the locket engraved, but it's engraved with an old pet name. The sort of thing a lover would know about."

Rena looked at me cockeyed. "Are you suggesting that the locket was a token from a lover? Because if so, that suggests that Pamela Rawlins and Mari Aames both had flings with the same man. The two women couldn't be any more different from each other. I can't imagine the man who would be attracted to both of them."

"I can," I said. "Phillip Denford. P.D. He was attracted to everything with two X chromosomes. Lord knows he ogled me enough when he came by Trendy Tails."

Jack stopped with his fork halfway to his mouth. "He did what?"

I smiled and patted his arm. "Easy, tiger. The man's already dead."

He grumbled but went back to eating his tart.

"Ah, but what did they see in Phillip Denford?" Rena asked.

"I don't know. He certainly wasn't my cup of tea. But Ruth Kimmey told me that there were rumors about Pamela and Phillip last year. I don't like to put too much stock in gossip—"

"Really?" Jack asked.

I scowled at him. "Really. On its own, I wouldn't

have thought there was anything to Ruth's rumor, but when you combine the rumor with the matching lockets and the inscription from "P.D. . . ."

Rena leaned back in her chair and reached out to clasp Jolly's hand. "If Pamela and Mari were both having affairs with Phillip Denford, that gives them matching motives to go along with their matching necklaces."

We all pitched in to clean up the detritus of our feast, and then Jolly and Rena took their leave.

Jack leaned against the kitchen counter, an enigmatic smile on his face.

"Do you have to get going?" I asked.

"Only if you want me to."

What did I want? Jack and I had been dating for several months, and we'd managed to become more physically comfortable around each other with every passing day. If I'd thought for an instant that Jack was looking for a cup of tea or a beer, I would have ushered him up to my apartment already. But that slow, hot smile coupled with the way his body had relaxed, like he didn't want to appear threatening, told me that Jack Collins was looking for more than tea.

It had been years since I'd been physically intimate with a man—since my fiancé, Casey, left me. I didn't know what to do.

Finally, something in me broke. I enjoyed the relationship Jack and I had built so far, but I wanted more. From him.

"Stay."

I took him by the hand and led him up the back stairs to my third-floor apartment. The dormer ceilings and small rooms made it difficult for a man Jack's size to negotiate the landscape, but he did his best.

We sat on my couch, a thrift-store find that I'd covered with patchwork pieces to hide the threadbare canvas beneath.

He slipped an arm around my shoulders and pulled me in so my cheek rested against his solid chest. I could hear the syncopated rhythm of his breath and his heartbeat.

"You're tense," he said. "You know you're safe, right? That I won't hurt you."

"Of course," I replied, lifting my head to look him in the eye. "I know you would never physically hurt me."

"Gee, thanks. I would have thought we could take that for granted. I didn't mean just physically. I meant what I said the other night. I love you. I will protect your heart as well as your body."

"Oh."

"You know I love you and you know I want you, but I'm the one who's in the dark here. Where do you see this relationship going? Do you love me back?"

I rested my head back down, more to hide from his

intense gaze than to cuddle. "You have to understand. I've made plans before, and they all fell apart. It's hard for me to forget that."

He pulled away, putting a little distance between us so I couldn't hide from his eyes. "But you have to. Casey was a fool to give you up, and he's gone now. I'm the man standing before you, pledging his love and asking for some sense of where our next steps will take us."

I took a deep breath. I thought of Ingrid and Dolly and Rena, throwing themselves into the fray of life, craving the good so much that they were unafraid of the potential heartache. "I . . . I care for you deeply. I think of you all the time. I'm happiest when I have you in my sights. If that's love, then I love you, too."

"And what do you want out of life? We've never talked about this, always just putting one foot in front of the other."

"I want to be happy. I'm not particular on how happy happens."

"Kids?"

"I think my mother would kill me if I didn't at least try. And, yeah, I think I would like to be a mom. You?"

"Oh, absolutely. I want to coach soccer and teach a kid to fish and help him with dioramas of dinosaurs for middle school science class."

I grinned. "What if you have a girl?"

"Same plan."

My grin melted into a giggle.

Jack pressed his fingertips to his forehead, eyes closed, like a medium receiving a message from the great beyond. "I think I see happiness in our future."

"How far in the future?" I teased.

"That's going to depend on a number of factors," Jack said, his voice a husky growl. He leaned forward to graze my earlobe with his teeth. "But let's get started soon."

CHAPTER
Thirteen

Mari Aames or Pamela Rawlins. That was the question.

The next day of the cat show brought with it a front from the south: low-hanging clouds, perpetual drizzle, and the occasional rumble of thunder from afar.

As soon as we got the booth set up, I went off in search of Pamela Rawlins, planning to pick her brain—subtly of course—about her relationship with Phillip Denford. I'd be having lunch with Pamela, Peter, Mari, and Marsha later that day, but I wanted to catch Pamela alone so I might catch her off guard.

I knew that the Siamese, Burmese, and Tonkinese cats were showing in ring six first thing that morning, so I headed in that direction, expecting to find Pamela showing Tonga. The ring was packed, but I thought tall, black-clad Pamela would stick out.

I was wrong. Pamela was nowhere to be found.

On my way back to the Trendy Tails booth, I swung by Ruth Kimmey's table to ask if she'd seen Pamela that day. I noticed that Ranger had accrued a number of multicolored ribbons that were now attached to his hutch.

"Pamela?" Ruth asked.

"Yeah. I thought she'd be showing Tonga, but she's not at the ring."

"Oh, she can't show Tonga," Ruth said, chin tucked to keep her words from traveling.

"Why not? He's a beautiful cat. I thought that was the whole purpose of her helping coordinate this show."

Ruth clucked softly. "No, ma'am. Tonga is a beautiful cat and was building up enough points to be a grand champion, but then he bit a judge."

"No!"

"Yes. Burmese are playful cats. The judge was trying to engage Tonga, but she was using a cat toy held between her finger and her thumb instead of one on a dangle. Tonga went for the toy, but got the judge's finger instead."

"So he wasn't aggressive or anything. Just playing."

"Doesn't matter. Phillip banned the cat from competition. Tonga's strictly a pet now."

"If she's not showing Tonga, why is Pamela even here? I haven't seen her with another cat."

Ruth shook her head. "No. No other cat. She's here in her capacity as a breeder."

"I didn't know she ran a cattery."

"Oh my, yes. Exotipaws. She breeds both Burmese and Tonkinese. I've tried to tell her to stop bringing Tonga to competitions, but she just won't listen to me."

"Why should she leave him at home?"

"Because he comes from her cattery and, rightly or wrongly, he's been banned from show for being overly aggressive. That cat is a constant reminder to potential buyers that Exotipaws cats are a gamble."

"I still can't believe I didn't know about her breeding business."

"As I said, Pamela is not the best businesswoman. The cat-breeding business is largely word of mouth, and that's not doing her any favors. She's already got a strike against her because she's so unpleasant to be around. What's more, she hasn't come up with a strategy to separate herself from the biting incident and, in fact, keeps making matters worse by carrying Tonga everywhere she goes. I've told her again and again: no one wants a biter. I can't imagine she's making much money off of her breeding operations."

"So if she's not showing and she's not a reputable breeder, why on earth did Phillip Denford put her in charge?"

"Pamela has been lobbying to coordinate one of the annual shows for years now. I think that's one of the

big reasons she had her little fling with Phillip, to butter him up. Phillip's not really the sentimental type, so
I can't imagine that swayed his mind any.

"To be perfectly honest, I think Pamela may have
blackmailed him just a scooch. Not that their affair—
or any of Phillip's affairs—was really secret, but there
are secrets and there are secrets, you know?"

"No."

"Well, for example, we all know most politicians
are corrupt, but we let it slide. But when there's a news
story about one of them doing a specific corrupt thing,
we get all mad about it. It was that way with Phillip's
affairs. As long as he was discreet, everyone else—and
I mean everyone else—was willing to be discreet, too.
Act like it didn't really happen. But if Pamela came
forward, no one would be able to deny the truth anymore. The M-CFO would be forced to confront Phillip's . . . lapses, shall we say. There would have been
an outcry to have him step down as chair of the committee."

"I get it."

"What's more, it would mean that Marsha Denford
couldn't keep pretending she didn't know either.
She'd have to decide whether to publicly support a
cheating spouse or get a divorce."

With that, Pamela Rawlins's motive shriveled. If
she'd had the affair to get the position of coordinating
the cat show, she'd gotten what she wanted. And if

she wanted anything else from him, the threat of exposure would be her currency. There was certainly no need to kill the man.

That left Mari as my prime suspect . . . the young girl having a fling with her boss. But how would that fling lead to motive for murder? I'd have to keep pressing if I hoped to find out.

Red, White & Bleu was Merryville's newest restaurant, the creation of erstwhile caterer Ken West. I wasn't the biggest fan of Ken—though he had been good to and good for my dear friend Taffy, who had started dating him about the same time I started dating Jack—but the restaurant was a huge asset to our little historic neighborhood. Ken served steaks, chops, hearty salads, and delicious home-style desserts in a relaxed, publike environment. I tended to have my favorites at the various eateries in town, and at Red, White & Bleu, I could happily devour a dish of their truffled mac and cheese and a slice of their house-made raspberry-studded almond pound cake every day of the week.

I met Peter, Marsha, and Pamela at the restaurant. As soon as we took our seats around the rough-hewn pine table, I realized that I was a bit of an outsider. These people weren't all just involved in the cat show; they were part of Phillip Denford's inner circle.

"How nice you could join us," Marsha said, the slight slur in her words unmistakable.

"Yes. I'm surprised to see you here." Pamela didn't sound surprised. She sounded annoyed.

"Peter invited me," I said, laying my napkin in my lap and leaning back so the server could fill my glass with water from a large glass pitcher he left on the table.

Peter smiled at Pamela. "I've been talking to Izzy here about theartisanway.com."

"Oh?" Pamela responded.

"Yes." Peter caught my eye. "Pamela was one of the first artists to sign up for the Web site. She is an amazing quilter."

"Really? I'd love to see your work sometime," I offered.

"It's on the Web site."

Okay, so Pamela did not have the warm fuzzies for me. I couldn't imagine why she would be upset that Peter had invited me to consider selling my wares on his Web site. Unless she was an owner? But even then, one would think she'd want more storefronts on the site, and the marketability of my product had been proven in my brick-and-mortar store.

Maybe she just didn't like me. To be fair, I might not like me either, if I were her.

"Your town is really quite lovely," Marsha said, breaking the sudden, inexplicable tension.

"Thank you," I said. "I may be a little partial since

I grew up here, but I actually like living here better than I did in Madison."

"How long were you in Madison?" Peter asked.

"Eight years," I responded. The number always took me by surprise. My time in Madison seemed so brief and long ago, yet Casey and I had been there for a significant percentage of our lives. "I went to the U and then stuck around while my then-fiancé attended medical school."

"Are you a small-town girl, then, coming home after so long in the big city?" There was a note of condescension in Marsha's voice, but I chose to ignore it.

"I never really thought of myself as a small-town girl. I had plans to move to New York, in fact. But Merryville now caters to such an upscale tourist trade that we have all the amenities of a big city but without the traffic."

Marsha and Peter chuckled politely, but I couldn't even get Pamela to crack a smile.

"I have to admit," Peter said, "when Pamela reported back to my father that this might be a suitable town for the M-CFO's silver anniversary, I thought she might have lost her mind." Pamela blinked at him slowly, clearly not amused. "But I've been pleasantly surprised."

"Me too," Marsha said. "Why, your little coffee shop . . . What is it called?"

"Joe Time," Peter said.

"Right. So clever. Joe Time. They make their own flavored syrups, and I've been able to keep up my lavender latte habit. It's the hot new flavor, you know."

Peter shivered theatrically. "I don't know how you can muck up perfectly good coffee with all that milk and sugar and candy flavoring."

Marsha reached across the table to bat playfully at his arm. "We can't all be coffee purists like you, Peter."

"Sorry I'm late." Mari Aames bustled up to the table and slid into the last remaining chair. "I had some things to take care of."

"Really, darling?" Marsha oozed. "Are we working you too hard?"

Mari flushed. "No. It was, actually, uh, personal."

I fought to keep my hand from trembling as I took a sip of my water. I knew where Mari had been. She'd been having coffee with Jack. For more than two hours. Jack had assured me I had no reason to be jealous, and I trusted him more than I trusted myself, but a little corner of my mind wondered just how personal that coffee date had been.

"So maybe we're not working you hard enough?" Marsha asked with a small smile.

"I . . . uh . . . You know I love working for you, Mrs. Denford. I love being busy. I promise. I just needed to pop out to pick up a couple of things. It only took a couple of minutes."

"Oh, relax, Mari," Pamela said. Her patience for the younger woman seemed especially short.

"Yes, relax dear," Marsha crooned. "I am just teasing you. You've been working yourself ragged the last week. You're entitled to have a few hours to yourself."

I wondered about Mari's comment about working for Marsha Denford. I'd been operating under the assumption that she was Phillip's girl Friday and that she had little to do with Marsha. It seemed that Phillip's death had changed Mari's employment situation pretty dramatically. The question was whether Mari would rather report to Phillip or to Marsha.

When the server came to take Mari's order, he brought a round of prosecco to the table. "Compliments of the house," he said.

I looked to the bar and saw Ken standing there, a portfolio open in front of him, a pencil poised in his hand. He raised the other hand in a jaunty salute, and I waved back.

"How lovely," Marsha exclaimed.

"Yes. Ken West, the proprietor, is a friend." Of our own accord, he and I probably wouldn't have had much to do with each other, but thanks to his romance with Taffy, we were friends-ish—by default.

Once the glasses were passed around, I raised mine in toast. "To Phillip. May he rest in peace."

"To Phillip," the others muttered, and then there was a moment of silence as we all sipped at the bubbly.

As we set our glasses down, I saw that Peter, Pamela, and Marsha had drained their glasses in a single gulp, while Mari and I had each taken only a sip. You could tell who at the table actually had to work that afternoon.

"If it's not too painful," I said, "what was Phillip like? I met him a few times during the planning of the show, but those meetings were brief and all business."

Peter cocked his head and smiled at me. "*All* business?"

"Yes. I mean, for me the show is all business."

"Mmmm-hmmm."

"My husband was a shrewd man. He had a passion for cats and for business, and he didn't mess around with either one," Martha said.

We put the reminiscing on hold then while the server passed around our orders. I didn't eat meat, but I could appreciate the rich aroma of Marsha's lamb chops and Peter's shepherd's pie. Outstate Minnesota caught a lot of guff for bland, unsophisticated food, but everything on the table looked like it could have come from a high-end restaurant in Minneapolis or Chicago.

As I tucked in to my mac and cheese, a homely dish elevated by the use of an especially sharp aged cheddar and earthy truffle oil, I thought about what Marsha had said. *Shrewd*. That struck me as an odd adjective for a woman to use to describe her newly departed husband. So unsentimental. But given that Phillip seemed to have been something of a cad, too, I could imagine that their relationship had not been as romantic as most other marriages.

Peter's smile spread into a grin. "Well put, Marsha."

The happier Peter seemed, the more annoyed Pamela got. "I was honored that he trusted me with coordinating the show this year. He had high standards, and being chosen to lead the twenty-fifth anniversary of the show meant the world."

Mari narrowed her eyes. "He let you pick the place, Pamela. Everything else, he left for me to decide. I'm the one he trusted. He might have given you the title of coordinator, but I'm the one who actually made all the arrangements. He didn't even let you see the design for the prize before the jeweler delivered it the first day of the show."

"Hush, now, Mari," Marsha crooned. "No one is doubting how much work you put into the show. We're all aware of what you did for my husband. Every last thing."

I got the sense that there was a whole lot more being communicated at that table than a simple observer such as myself could comprehend. The relationships between these people ran deep and, it seemed, so did the resentment. I wanted nothing so much as to crawl inside their heads and understand why Peter was so amused, why Pamela was so annoyed, why Mari was so defensive, and why Marsha was so . . . whatever Marsha was.

CHAPTER
Fourteen

As much as that pound cake was calling my name, I didn't think I could stand much more of the odd company and fraught atmosphere, so I asked for my check and scooted out of the Red, White & Bleu as soon as I'd swallowed the last of my mac and cheese.

After that awkward lunch, I decided that I was so close to home it would almost be a crime not to stop by the store to check in on Wanda and maybe take poor, neglected Packer for a walk. It would be good for Wanda, good for the dog, and good for me.

When I walked in, I found Wanda actually helping a customer—a woman with a rat terrier on a leash, who seemed to be interested in purchasing him a trench coat. Because the coats were made to order,

Wanda was kneeling on the ground, trying to take the wiggly dog's measurements.

"Hi," I said, extending a hand to the dog owner. "I'm Izzy McHale. I'm the owner."

The woman smiled and took my hand. "So nice to meet you! I love your store."

"Thanks."

Wanda had hooked our jerry-rigged tape measure to the dog's collar and was stretching it down his back, trying to keep it straight down his spine.

"I'm Sandra Lowe." She tugged gently on the terrier's leash. "Savage, here, and I just moved to town from Detroit. Well, and we brought my husband and youngest daughter, too."

"Detroit? My gracious, that's a long way. What brings you to Merryville?"

"Retirement."

"Really?"

"I know," she said with a laugh. "Our friends all think we're crazy, moving north instead of south. But my husband, Jesse, and I are avid outdoorsmen. We like to cross-country ski, snowmobile, hunt, fish, hike . . . you name it. Minnesota is like paradise. We were all set to move into one of the units at The Woods at Badger Lake, but Mr. Olson let us know a couple of months ago that there was a slight delay in getting the units move-in ready. We decided we didn't want to wait until next spring, so we rented a place just outside of town and here we are!"

Dear heavens. A couple of months ago? Hal Olson, our mayor and the man who founded The Woods at Badger Lake, had known since April that the whole project was on hold and might not ever get started again. Yet he hadn't told these investors—these *buyers*—that there was even a delay until a couple of months ago? That was nuts.

"So you already bought a condo?"

"Oh, yes. We came out last summer to see the site and fell in love with the lake. And Merryville. We bought unit number one!"

Last summer. Hal Olson hadn't even owned the land for the development the summer before. He hadn't bought it until October. If he was showing people the property before he owned it and selling condos that weren't built, he was definitely putting the cart before the horse. But, of course, he'd probably needed those first few condo sales in order to pay the contractors who were doing the work. . . . I was no business wiz, but the whole situation seemed pretty sketchy to me.

"Have you been out to see the unit since you got to town?" I asked carefully.

"No, not yet." Sandra frowned. "We've touched base with Hal a couple of times, but he's so busy with being mayor and all, it's been hard to pin him down."

Yeah. Busy being mayor. I was certain that wasn't the only reason Hal was ducking the Lowes' calls. He couldn't very well drive them out to the site by the lake and let them see the piles of wood and rebar sitting idly in the sun. But it wasn't my place to let this woman know that her future home was currently an abandoned construction site.

"And now I read in the *Merryville Gazette* that Hal's wife, Pris, may be in some sort of legal trouble. Something about a theft and a murder? We met Pris when we came to visit last summer, and it just doesn't seem possible that she could be involved with anything so . . . so criminal."

"We're all hoping that matter gets cleared up soon," I said.

"You're a local. Is there anything we should be concerned about?"

They ought to be concerned about the fact that they'd picked up their lives and moved three states over relying on a condo that might never be built. But, again, I couldn't bring myself to tell Sandra that.

"I promise the trouble with Pris is nothing to be concerned about," I hedged.

"I should certainly hope so. I don't want to sound selfish, but we'd really like to see our condo, and I don't imagine we'll be able to pull Hal from his wife's side while she's in this predicament."

Funny thing was, while Pris was in this predicament, Hal seemed perfectly content to keep his distance.

"How old's your daughter?" I asked, trying to steer the conversation away from The Woods at Badger Lake.

"Krista will be a senior in the fall. She's not happy with us for moving her away from her high school before her very last year," Sandra confessed.

"Wanda here will be a senior this fall, too. Maybe she can take your Krista under her wing."

Wanda cast me a sidelong glare before smiling up at Sandra. "Happy to do it!"

I didn't exactly follow the social machinations at Merryville High, but I knew enough to know that Wanda was one of the popular kids. She had long hair, brown at the roots and much lighter at the ends. Lucy said the coloring technique was called "ombré," just like the fabric-dyeing technique, and assured me it was very expensive. Wanda had hinted that she'd taken the job at Trendy Tails only to keep her hair in the latest style and to have plenty of money for those few luxuries her parents wouldn't splurge on.

No matter how great Sandra's daughter was, I'd basically asked Wanda to take on a charity case, and I knew I'd be paying for it somehow.

While Wanda finished taking Savage's measurements, I wished Sandra every happiness in Merryville and then dashed up the stairs to retrieve Packer from his kennel. I was on my way down the back stairs, so as to avoid any potential confrontation between Savage and Packer, when Ingrid popped out onto the second-floor landing.

"I was talking to Rena," Ingrid said, "and she filled me in a little more on your predicament. You know, you used to confide everything in me," she chided.

I wrapped her in a quick hug. "I wasn't trying to keep anything from you. It's just all so complicated, and you have a lot on your plate right now."

"I may have cancer, but I'm not an invalid yet. Rena told me that that man, Phillip Denford? Is that his name?" I nodded. "She said that he was threatening your business. I hope all that's cleared up now that he's dead, but if you're still in trouble, I'm here to help."

"You've already helped me more than I could have ever expected, Ingrid."

"You don't expect enough. Like I said, I think of you like my own child. If Trendy Tails goes under—and I'm not saying it will, because I know you run a good business here—but if it does, your aunt Dolly and I want to go halvsies on setting you up in a new business. I know it wouldn't be as fun as making clothes for the cats and dogs. You have a real knack for that. But you also have the talent to make clothes for people. Rena told me about the Swag and Wags idea of selling matching pet/owner clothing, and I think it's a splendid idea. But if that twist isn't enough to keep the pet boutique open, we're willing to finance a new boutique for you, a fresh start where you can sell whatever you want to sell. If it comes to that. Which it won't."

I stood there speechless, so deeply moved that my mentor and my aunt would conspire to develop a backup plan for me.

"You'd just have to promise me you'll keep Rena on board. Because I like that girl. I don't care what all those stuffy ladies at Methodist Ladies' Auxiliary say about her."

A bubble of laughter escaped my lips. "I like that girl, too. She's not going anywhere. And neither is Trendy Tails. Or Swag and Wags, if we go that route. I don't know how far Phillip had gotten in his plans to run me out of business. I don't know whether the people who operate his business or his heirs even know about the plan, much less whether they're going to carry through with it, but I know that I won't let them succeed."

"Good for you."

"But, Ingrid?"

"Yes, dear?"

"You are the greatest friend a girl could have—you know that? I don't know where I'd be without you. I don't know how I'm going to keep pushing forward without you here to help me."

It was her turn to embrace me. "Izzy, I haven't helped

you. I've just given you the occasional opportunity. You've taken every one and turned it into a success by your own hard work and smarts."

She patted me on the back, good solid thumps that reminded me of what a strong woman she was. I wanted to be strong to honor her, so I pushed down even the hint of tears before I stepped away and led Packer out the back door.

But all the while I stayed strong on the inside, my heart melted at the joy of knowing true generosity.

It was a beautiful day for a walk. A front was moving in, promising rain and possibly storms to come, but that day the weather was a balmy seventy-eight degrees. The sky glowed the blue of shallow Caribbean waters with lacy swaths of clouds pushed by a gentle breeze. It was about as good as it got for Minnesota in August.

Packer and I picked our way through the alley behind Trendy Tails, making our way past the backs of the Greene Brigade, Joe Time, Taffy's Happy Leaf, and Red, White & Bleu before emerging on the street. As usual, Packer had to stop and sniff everything in sight.

Packer had originally belonged to my fiancé, Casey Alter. Casey had named the pooch after his favorite football team and swore he'd take care of the dog. But, alas, as a medical resident, Casey didn't have the time to devote to such an energetic beastie, so I was the primary caregiver for our little Packer. When Casey ran off to New York with his former mistress and new love, he couldn't take Packer with him. The new girl, Rachel, didn't like Packer because he sneezed and snuffled and sometimes drooled a little. By that point, I'd bonded with the little fella enough that I was relieved when Casey asked me to keep him.

But Rachel was right that Packer was a handful.

As we walked past the back of Richard Greene's military memorabilia shop, Packer pulled me to the left so he could sniff all around the bricks and trash cans for any scent of Richard's dog. Then he found a little lump of unidentifiable stuff, and I had to tug him hard to keep him from playing with it. Finally, as we reached the end of the alley, he was assailed by the smell of baked goods emanating from my friend Taffy's tea shop and the rich smells wafting through the kitchen door of Red, White & Bleu.

He stood there, backside waggling in doggy bliss but totally unable to decide which direction offered the best chance at goodies. He'd start for Red, White & Bleu, then stop, turn in place three times, and start to trip over his tangled leash to get to the back door of Taffy's Happy Leaf.

Finally, I gave in and fished one of Rena's home-made dog biscuits out of my jeans pocket and offered it to Packer, using it like a carrot, held just out of reach, to lure him out of the alley. Then I dropped to one knee and let him eat the biscuit from my hand. In Packer's world, smells are nice, but food is better. He crunched and gulped and the biscuit was gone in a flash.

We walked the couple of blocks to Dakota Park at a good, brisk clip, in part so I could get back to the show to relieve Rena and in part to burn off a little of my mac-and-cheese lunch.

Dakota Park was the social hub of Merryville. It was surrounded on all sides by residential neighborhoods, businesses, the courthouse, and a church. The park itself boasted a big playground, an area with picnic tables, and a gazebo-like band shell. It played host to the annual Halloween Howl, a Holiday Winterfest, a Spring Fling, and, of course, the annual fireworks display on the Fourth of July. Between these major events, the park constantly hummed with children and dogs and spirited conversation.

I took Packer to his favorite spot, a bench by the playground, and was pleasantly surprised to find Ama Olmstead there with her son, Jordan. He was a beautiful boy, with deep brown hair, chocolate-drop eyes, and rosy cherub cheeks. As an added bonus, he and Packer got along great.

"Izzy! Good to see you."

"Hi, Ama. Enjoying the weather?"

"It's one of the best things about working from

home. I can keep my own hours, and when a lovely, sunny day rolls around, Jordan and I can take full advantage."

"How's work at the paper?"

"Well, you know. Print journalism is a tough business these days. I think we actually have it better in the small towns. Our local news doesn't get picked up on the local network affiliates as often, so if you want to know what's happening in Merryville, you pretty much have to read the *Gazette*. The problem we're facing is shifting to an online format, which people are demanding, and still keeping them paying for content. People want their news on a screen, but when they see it there, it doesn't seem as valuable."

"Huh."

She laughed. "Short answer, everything's fine."

For a few moments we watched as Jordan greeted Packer, wrapping his chubby little arms around the dog's neck, Packer twisting and leaping in the boy's grip, obviously delighted with his company. When Packer took a couple of steps backward, Jordan rocked up onto his knees, his bum in the air, and giggled with glee.

"How about you?" Ama asked. "You, um, dealing okay with Phillip Denford's murder?"

I narrowed my eyes at her. "Fine. Why do you ask?"

"I hear things," she said with a shrug. "I know the

police talked to you. That they may not be *done* talking
to you."

My heart sank. Ama was a reporter. If she'd heard
that the police considered me anything close to a suspect in Phillip's death, I was in terrible trouble.

"Don't worry," she said as though she read my
mind. "I owe you big. If the police take formal action,
I'll have to report on it. After all, if I don't, someone
else will . . . someone who may not be quite so interested in your side of the story. But as long as it was
just that one meeting with Gil, mum's the word."

"Thank you." Once again, I was overwhelmed at
the generosity of the people in my life. I was still on
thin ice with the law, but I felt like I found support
everywhere I turned.

"What do you think happened?" Ama asked. She
held up a hand and smiled. "Purely off the record. I
swear."

"Honestly, I don't know. I've heard rumors that
Phillip had affairs with Pamela Rawlins and one of
the cat fanciers, a woman named Ruth Kimmey. The
affair with Ruth was a long time ago, though. My
source—if you can call her that—thinks that Pamela
slept with Phillip only to get the position of coordinator of the show, so her relationship with Phillip doesn't
seem like much of a motive, but Phillip also got one
of Pamela's cats banned from shows and, in the process, took a major bite out of her breeding business.

Mari Aames was having an affair with Phillip, too, but she seemed to worship the man. And I know that Phillip and his son, Peter, weren't exactly close, but I don't see that Peter had any real incentive to kill Phillip. In fact, Peter's starting a new business, and he's made references to a silent partner. I think it may have been his father."

I tugged on Packer's leash to keep him from actually standing on top of Jordan.

"In short, I can't find a single person who liked the man, other than the apparently lovelorn Mari, but I don't have any credible suspects for who would have wanted him dead except for me and Pris. And we didn't do it."

"Are you so sure about Pris?"

I explained that I'd seen Phillip that morning, though I left out our topic of conversation.

Ama shook her head. "You're assuming that she would have had to go all the way home to get changed out of any bloody clothes. But if she'd *planned* to kill Phillip that morning, she would have had a change of clothes on her. All she would have had to do was slip into the ladies' room and scrub up a bit."

Ama made an interesting point. Pris did carry around that huge tote bag, which could have easily hidden a spare outfit. Forget about getting to the ladies' room. Pris had a nice little secluded area for her grooming operation in the corner of the room. I suddenly remembered the flatiron that had skidded out of Pris's bag when it fell off her arm and disgorged the collar dangle. She could have even redone her hair after killing Phillip.

But if that was the case, if she'd committed the murder and then gotten cleaned up at the North Woods Hotel, why would she have left again as soon as the show got started? I didn't care what Jack said. If Pris had been at the show right before or after the blackout, I would have seen her.

"Listen," I said. "You were there that morning. When did you first see Pris?"

"Jeez, I don't know. It's hard to say. There was so much going on, and I wasn't paying particular attention to Prissy." She reached out a hand. "Jordan, give that rock to Mommy. We've talked about this before. Rocks are not food."

The little boy handed the rock to his mother and then blissfully returned to wrestling with my dog.

"Your pictures," I said. "Would you do me a huge favor and go back through the pictures you took that day? See when you first spot Pris and where she is at the time?"

Ama looked at me like I was nuts, but she nodded. "Like I said, Izzy. I owe you. I don't see what good it will do, but I'll look for you."

CHAPTER
Fifteen

By the time I got Packer back to Trendy Tails and my own self back to the cat show, Rena was about ready to kill me.

" 'Lunch,' you said. 'Doggy bag,' you said. Yet here I am at two in the afternoon, no lunch in sight."

"I'm so sorry. Lunch was so weird, I wanted to get out of there as soon as possible. I couldn't stand the thought of spending any more time with that crew, so I didn't want to stick around to wait for another order of mac and cheese."

"You had the mac and cheese? Ken's mac and cheese? Salt in the wound, my friend. Salt. In. The. Wound." She shook her head at me, deep disappointment in her eyes. "Besides, if you were in such an all-fired hurry to get out of there, why are you so late?"

"Because I took Packer for a little walk, which turned into a long conversation with Ama Olmstead. I have her going through the pictures she took the morning Phillip died to see what she can figure out about who was where and when. Especially the cagey Pris Olson."

"Izzy!"

I looked over my shoulder to find Ruth Kimmey bearing down on me from behind. "Izzy McHale, I have to talk to you. I have the most interesting bit of news."

Behind her, I saw Pamela, Mari, Marsha, and Peter, apparently just now returning from our lunch. They must have stayed for dessert. I raised a hand to wave hello, and Peter waved back. He looked pointedly between me and Ruth, reminding me without a word of our conversation about Ruth's wilder days.

I could feel the heat spreading across my face. Ruth frowned and glanced over her shoulder at the group of M-CFO bigwigs. Her frown deepened when she caught sight of our little lunch bunch.

"What's the news, Ruth?" I asked.

"Not here," she said. "Can you walk with me outside?"

I looked at Rena, who glowered back. "I've really got to man the booth while Rena takes a break and gets some lunch."

Ruth glanced down at her wrist, where her charm

bracelet hung. "Dang it. I always forget I don't wear a watch anymore. Stupid cell phones."

I pulled mine out of my pocket. "It's two fifteen."

"The finals of the agility competition will be starting at three. Do you think you can meet me out by the course around two forty-five?"

I looked at Rena, whose eyebrows were now completely flat. "Yes?" Rena rolled her eyes but nodded.

"Great. I'll get T.J. to watch Ranger, and I'll see you soon."

I didn't know what Ruth Kimmey had to tell me, but up until that point she'd been a font of valuable information. After all, she knew the cat-show attendees far better than I did, and her powers of observation would make her a better PI than my aunt Dolly could ever hope to be.

A sudden influx of business from a group of tabby owners who had just finished a conformation round kept me tied up at the Trendy Tails table for longer than I'd expected. Even with Rena back, I had to stick around to help, so I was late going to meet Ruth. I made my way out of the hotel's side door and down the gentle slope to the tent where the agility course remained in place. People were already gathering for the finals of the agility competition.

In a crowd full of women, I usually had a solid height advantage, but the agility competition seemed to attract more men, and a small herd of strapping Scandinavian men blocked my view. As politely as I could, I made my way toward the front of the crowd, searching for Ruth and earning myself a few choice curse words from the people I outmaneuvered.

I made it all the way to the front of the crowd, but still no Ruth.

Once again, my female lunch companions managed to project absolute contempt for one another as they sat at the judging table. Pamela consulted her phone for the time and called the group to order. The first contestant up was a younger woman, maybe in her late twenties. She wore a long cotton jersey skirt topped by a sleeveless tunic and a broad-brimmed sunhat on her head. Her cat, a gray tiger-striped tabby, wore a kelly green collar that matched his owner's hat to a tee.

The cat took its place at the starting line, and the young woman pulled a play wand out of a canvas knapsack. With a nod from Pamela, they were off.

The tabby went up the ramp, across the bridge, and down the ramp, through the first nylon tunnel, then out, then into the second nylon tunnel, and then . . . nothing. The young woman stood at the far end of the second tunnel, bobbing the cat toy and growing visibly more distressed by the second, but the cat didn't appear.

Instead, the tunnel started rocking and bulging, as though the cat were wrestling with something inside.

The young woman finally knelt down to see what had become of her feline friend. She gasped loudly and promptly passed out, her body pitching forward and bunching the nylon tunnel up around whatever was obstructing the cat's progress.

Only it wasn't a whatever at all. It was a whoever.

A delicate hand extended from the end of the tunnel. I immediately recognized the delicate charm bracelet dangling around the limp wrist. It was Ruth Kimmey.

That's when I noticed that the crossbar from the final hurdle in the course was not resting on its uprights. Instead, it lay next to the second nylon tunnel, one end of the white post smeared with red.

By that point, everyone in the crowd had cottoned on to what was happening. Another body in their midst. Another murder.

For my part, I felt a pang of sorrow at Ruth's passing. She'd been kind to me, showing me the ropes of the cat show and telling me what she knew of the players in this strange performance. And whatever her last bit of information had been, whatever had prompted her to invite me out to the agility field, she'd taken it to her grave.

I couldn't help but wonder if, had I been on time, I could have saved Ruth Kimmey's life.

It took the police a lot less time to clear the people from the crime scene the second time around. Most of the onlookers were already on file as witnesses in the first murder, and no one had seen a thing. At least, not that they would say aloud.

I went back inside as soon as I could. After stopping to tell Rena what little I knew, I made a beeline for Ruth's table. The police had cordoned it off already, leaving poor T. J. Leuzinger standing outside a ring of crime-scene tape, Cataclysm Ranger draped over her shoulder and tears pouring down her face.

"Oh, T.J. I'm so sorry for your loss," I said.

"Poor Ranger," she said, looking at me with a puzzled expression. "What happens to Ranger? Ruth's horrible husband had Ranger neutered just to hurt her. Ranger can't go live with him."

I hushed her softly and petted Ranger's head. "I don't think you have to worry, T.J. Ranger isn't their child. He doesn't just automatically get custody. Legally, Ranger is stuff and will belong to whoever is her heir."

"I don't know," she said, her voice approaching a hysterical pitch. "She never said. She doesn't have children. But I think she has a sister in Illinois."

"There you go. I bet Ranger will belong to the sister in Illinois. And if the sister doesn't want him, I'm sure she'll just let you have him. You'll take good care of him if it comes to that. Ranger's in good hands."

I made a mental note to have Sean draft my will.

I'd already had to take care of one murder victim's orphaned animal, and now seeing T.J. freaking out about what would happen to Ranger, I realized I should be responsible and make sure that there was a plan in place for Packer and Jinx if something should happen to me.

"T.J.," I said softly, "Ruth said she had something to tell me. I was supposed to meet her outside, where she died. It might be really important. Did she tell you what it was?"

"Something to tell you?" I could see the wheels spinning in T.J.'s mind. "Yes. Oh yes, she did say something. But it didn't make any sense."

"What was it?" I prodded.

"She'd run upstairs to get another sweater. You know, she would never just start the day dressed right and she always found herself cold. I don't know how many times I told her to just put on a sweater first thing in the morning—"

"T.J. She went to get a sweater, and . . ."

"Oh. Well, she came hustling back into the ballroom, no sweater to be seen, and told me she had to tell you something important. 'It's in the blood.' That's what she said she needed to tell you. 'It's in the blood.'"

"Did anyone else leave the ballroom at the same time Ruth did? Or thereabouts?"

"I honestly wasn't paying attention. Right before

Ruth left, the two of us had been talking with Marsha about plans for next year's show. It won't be nearly as elaborate as this, but Marsha's determined to make it special in honor of Phillip. Anyway, she'd just left to take her afternoon nap when Ruth decided to get her sweater."

"Afternoon nap?"

"Oh yes, every day. Marsha's not a well woman. I would never say this to her face, but I think she should limit her travels with Phillip and stay home to rest. And I don't think it's the best idea for her to take on the major task of organizing next year's show. That will take a lot out of her."

"What, exactly, is wrong with her?"

"I don't know."

I suspected I did: clonazepam and the occasional cocktail. That would certainly explain the need for a nap.

T.J. shifted Ranger on her shoulder.

"Do you want me to hold him for a while?"

She sighed and offered me a watery smile. "That would be great." She placed the cat in my arms. I was so used to holding Jinx, my sweet, massive kitty, that Ranger felt insubstantial as I held him against me.

"T.J.? Do you know much about Mari Aames?" It was a long shot, but since we were standing there shooting the breeze . . .

"Oh, Mari. Bless her heart, but Phillip runs her ragged. Or I guess he did run her ragged. Now it will be up to Marsha to keep her employed. Frankly, I don't know why she's worked for the Denfords as long as she has. They pay her a pittance."

I leaned in close. "I heard a rumor that Mari and Phillip were, you know . . ."

At first T.J. just stared at me, but then she caught on and laughed. "I can see where people might think that. After all, everyone knows Phillip had a wandering eye, and Mari was positively dazzled by him. But I was talking to Phillip the day before he died, and he said that he was planning to let Mari go after the show."

I was stunned. "Really? But she seems to do such a wonderful job."

T.J. shrugged and reached out to take Ranger back. "He hinted that her adoration was a little much. That she was too clingy. I saw her in the bathroom that same day, vomiting and weeping after Phillip had criticized some decision she'd made. I think Phillip needed an assistant made of stronger stuff."

T.J. cuddled Ranger like a baby and began idly rubbing his tummy, eliciting a deep, rumbling purr from the cat. "Come to think of it," T.J. mused, "I saw Mari running out of here at about the same time Ruth went up to her room. I can't remember whether it was before or after, but she had her hand over her mouth and looked to be fighting back tears. Some other crisis, I suppose."

It's in the blood. Something Ruth saw or heard during the last hours of her life led her to that cryptic statement. And got her killed.

CHAPTER
Sixteen

"What the heck does that mean?" Sean asked.

"I don't know. I'm thinking it must have something to do with breeding."

"Breeding?" He took a sip of Taffy's chamomile mint tea. "Like cat breeding?"

"Yeah."

The police had insisted on shutting down the cat show for the rest of the day. I'd left Jack back at the North Woods Hotel, working with his crew to sort through whatever evidence they might find, and had asked Sean to meet me at the Happy Leaf for scones and herbal tea: something to soothe my nerves after a long and emotional day.

"Why on earth would anyone care enough about cat breeding to kill someone?"

"There's a lot of money involved. Not to mention pride. T. J. Leuzinger was about to have a breakdown after she heard about Ruth's death, and I think a good chunk of her emotion had to do with Ranger's fate rather than Ruth's. She didn't even own Ranger anymore, but she acted like she was basking in the cat's reflected glory."

Sean tore off a corner of a lemon cream scone. "So which breeder would want Phillip dead?" he asked before popping the tidbit in his mouth.

"I'm guessing Phillip made plenty of enemies along the way, but I know that he basically destroyed Pamela Rawlins's breeding business by blackballing her Tonga from the show circuit. It meant that Tonga was no longer a viable sire, and it cast a cloud of doubt on her entire breeding operation. I think Ruth's comments move Pamela to the top of our suspect list."

I took a sip of my tea. It was tasty, but still a little bitter for me. I added another spoonful of sugar. I looked up to find Sean smiling at me.

"What?"

"You have such a sweet tooth."

"Look who's talking."

His smile widened. "I know. I need Rena to bake for me more. Do you think she'd start me on a regular rotation of her banana bread and her chocolate-chocolate-chip cookies if I asked her pretty please?"

I clinked my spoon against the side of my cup to

shake off any excess liquid. "I think she'd do just about anything you asked her to do. That girl adores you."

"And you?"

"And me, what?" I said.

"Do you adore me?"

"Sean. That's not fair."

His smile disappeared. "Right. And life is always fair."

"I don't want to start this."

"Of course not. On the one hand, you can't keep your nose out of everyone's business. But on the other, when the spotlight is on you, you become completely nonconfrontational. You don't want to face anything ugly."

"Seriously? Sean, after the day I've had, I cannot possibly have this fight with you. I need you to support me right now."

"Yes, you certainly do."

"What's that supposed to mean?"

Sean frowned at me, and for a second I thought I saw a flash of fear in his eyes. "I got a call from Gil Dixon right after you called me this afternoon. He'd heard that you were buying the property at 801 Maple, and he suggested the cops were going to get a subpoena for your financial records."

"So? There's nothing hinky with my financial records, unless hovering on the edge of broke is hinky."

Trendy Tails was doing reasonably well, but every penny of profit was going back into the business, and I took only enough salary to get by.

"That's the problem. How does someone with no money expect to buy a well-constructed, recently renovated three-story house?"

I shook my head before taking a sip of my now-sweet tea. "Ingrid's selling me the place for a song."

"I know that, and you know that, and eventually the police will know that. But for now they're going to look at that apparent anomaly and wonder. The very fact that they're bothering with your financials means that someone—at the very least Gil Dixon and possibly someone in the county attorney's office—still considers you a viable suspect for the theft of the collar dangle. And they're only looking at you for the theft because you have a motive for the murder."

"But now it's clearly not me. Ruth's death proves it."

Sean popped another bite of scone in his mouth. "It proves no such thing. Another person you were close with is dead. Pris never even spoke to Ruth, but you have been attached to the woman's hip."

"That's not true," I said. "Pris said she'd been speaking to Ruth right before the lights went out on the day of Phillip's murder. She did know Ruth."

"Who told you that?"

"Pris."

"Well, someone's lying, then. I'd just heard about Ruth's death, so I asked Gil about Ruth's statement the day of Phillip's murder. Ruth told the police that she'd run up to her room to get a sweater. The lights were on when she left and on when she got back. She wasn't talking to anyone when those lights went out. In fact, the police think that that may be why she was killed: that she may have unwittingly seen the person who tripped the breakers out in the hallway on her way up to her room."

I swallowed hard. "Maybe that's exactly why she was murdered," I said. "Maybe she saw Pamela or Mari out in that hallway and had just realized the significance of what she'd seen."

Sean set his cup down hard enough to rattle its saucer.

Taffy looked up from the counter, where she'd been quietly humming while she piped frosting on her famous tea cookies. "You two okay?"

"Fine, Taffy. Just got a little carried away," I said.

Sean forced a smile. "Sorry about that."

She went back to her piping.

"Listen, I don't really care what Ruth saw or didn't see. I don't care what she said, what she thought, or why she died. What I care about is you, and I want you to stay away from that cat show."

"What?"

"Two people are dead, and you've managed to become a suspect in both murders . . . not to mention the theft. Somehow your efforts to solve this case are making you look guiltier by the second. And then there's the danger. Let's say Ruth was killed because she saw something. She was killed where and when she was supposed to meet you. Do you realize how close you could have come to being hurt?"

"Okay, Sean. I get it. I'm not actually trying to get into more trouble here. I'll do my best to lie low. I promise."

He offered me a grudging smile, and I returned it with all the warmth I could muster.

I had every intention of keeping that promise. I swear I did.

Later that day, I decided to take Jinx in to be groomed at Pris's brick-and-mortar store so she'd be looking her best for the cat show. While Jinx was infinitely tolerant of me dressing her up in all sorts of outfits, she did not handle baths well. It was likely my fault. I'd always considered cats to be self-cleaning creatures, so she wasn't used to being forced to stand in water while having more dumped over her head. Those rare times when she needed assistance with her ablutions, it had not gone well. Jinx was a big girl, and I had a hard time wrestling her in a bathtub. Always, she shot her four legs out to brace herself on the sides of the tub, making it impossible to get her down to the level of the water.

Frankly, I had an ulterior motive for bringing Jinx in for grooming. I was hoping to run into Pris at her store, too. Since Phillip's death, she'd avoided the cat show, and I really wanted to talk with her. Luckily, she was working the front desk. Even though she was alone in the salon, she wore a pale pink twinset with an A-line khaki skirt, a string of pearls at her throat and a diamond tennis bracelet gracing her wrist.

"I've decided to enter Jinx in the household-pet division of the show."

"Really? That seems so unlike you."

Normally, I would have spent a few seconds reading into that statement, trying to parse out if there was a jab in there or not. Instead, I responded right away: "I know, right?"

"So what's prompting all of this?"

"Well, Ruth Kimmey was saying . . . Ruth is one of the—"

"I met Ruth."

"Right, well, she was saying that Jinx has great coloring and all the markers of a prizewinning Norwegian forest cat. And I thought, why not? I won't be hurt if she loses. Either way, it will be a great story. You only live once, after all."

"Isn't that the truth?"

"So do you have time for a quick groom?"

Pris craned her neck to look around the empty store. "Yes. I think I can fit you in."

She took Jinx's crate and lifted it over the counter that separated her from her clients. "To be honest, I'm losing my mind working here all alone. It's been so quiet. Would you be willing to stick around and keep me company for a bit?"

"Me?"

Pris smiled a soft, secret smile. "Come on. Don't act so shocked. I know we don't usually move in the same social circles, but we are in the same profession."

Not to mention that Pris's own social circle had all but given her the boot at that point.

"And it's true you've accused my husband of murder. Twice. But I think giving me an alibi this go-around more than makes up for that."

I laughed at her lopsided math.

I followed her around the counter and into the back of the shop. While the front of Pris's store was all luxury—heavy carpets, gold-framed mirrors, gilt shelves lined with high-end grooming products—the back was where the action happened. There looked to be six stations, each with a sink and a long extender hose like my hairdresser used, a table with a stand for hooking collars, and a dryer box. It was utilitarian but pristine, sparkling with white and chrome.

"So have the police backed off you for Phillip's murder?"

Pris laughed. "You don't mince words, do you?"

"Hey, we're both smack in the middle of this thing."

"I guess so." She sighed. "They went through all my inventory of grooming shears to confirm what I'd already told them: I only use Cutsright grooming products. The shears that killed Phillip were Guttenheim. I have no problem with Guttenheim shears, but I get a better discount through Cutsright. So the shears that killed Phillip weren't mine. That seems to have helped a little."

"A little?"

She took Jinx out of her cage and dropped her into the sink. Jinx, being the generally chill cat she was, seemed perfectly fine hanging out there, though something told me she'd be less happy when the water came on.

Pris reached for a pair of elbow-length rubber gloves, much thicker than the kind I used in my own kitchen. Before putting them on, she spun around and leaned against the sink. She raised her hand to stroke her pearls, but then flinched and dropped the hand to the gloves again.

"They're still after me hard about the stolen collar dangle. I've told them I have no idea how it ended up in my purse, but of course that's falling on deaf ears.

'Yeah, right, lady.' And then," she said with a sigh, "there's my great big fat motive for killing the man."

"Motive? Does this have anything to do with the fight you had the night before he died?"

Pris narrowed her eyes, sizing me up. "I guess you'll hear all about this from your great big hunk of a detective. Nice job, by the way."

She made my relationship with Jack sound so calculating. I couldn't muster up the will to thank her.

"Well, here's the thing," Pris said. "Phillip's death made Hal's and my life so much better."

Pris was married to Hal Olson. He was one of those guys who everyone thought was slightly shady, always trying to put together some kind of deal (preferably a deal that brought him money). Still, he'd managed to get himself elected mayor of Merryville, and he hadn't bankrupted the town yet.

"How did Phillip's death help you two?"

"A few months ago, Marsha—who's a lovely woman, by the way—talked Phillip into serving as an angel investor for The Woods at Badger Lake. He provided us with the capital to keep the contractors at bay while we fought the Department of Natural Resources on the whole rare-owl-habitat brouhaha. But in exchange for Phillip's financial support, Hal gave him a fifty-percent share in the project. Just last week, we got some good news from our lawyer. It looked like the DNR was going to relocate the burrowing owls so we could continue to build. But we were tapped out. Like, we didn't have enough money to pay our mortgage for one more month."

"Wow. I didn't know it was that bad, Pris."

"That was sort of the point. We had to try to keep up the impression that we were fine financially to prevent our creditors from swooping in like a bunch of vultures."

I didn't bother to tell her that everyone in town knew they were struggling.

"The ruling from the DNR was right there, so close we could taste it, but we couldn't hold out another day. Phillip offered to buy out Hal's shares in the project for pennies on the dollar. It would have stopped us from hemorrhaging cash and it would have paid the month's mortgage, but it would have cut Hal off from any of the profits from the project."

"Denford really was a snake."

"Snake doesn't begin to cover it. He'd structured the original deal with Hal to leave open this possibility, and Hal had been so eager for the cash he hadn't thought about all the consequences. He thought that we were all friends, the Denfords and the Olsons. They had us over to their house for dinner. We drove three hours just to get there. We toasted with champagne. Hal never considered that for Phillip the whole deal was straight business."

"But how did Denford dying help?"

"Denford never started the purchase process. He'd drafted papers, shown them to Hal, but he hadn't taken any steps to execute the agreement. When he died, everything froze. His personal assets will be held until his estate goes through probate, and he played everything so close to the vest that he never informed his business manager of the deal. Hal was able to point to Phillip's death to buy us a little time with our creditors, and the DNR announced its decision to let us continue construction yesterday. Basically, we're saved."

I wondered if I was saved, too. Had Phillip already signed contracts to produce the knockoffs of my clothes? He'd said the cat pj's he brought in were just prototypes. Maybe his death would put an end to his plan to destroy my business.

"Anyway, the night before Phillip was killed, we had a fight about his plans to force Hal out. Crazy me, I thought I could talk him into being a human being. The whole situation gave me reason to kill Phillip *and* reason to steal the jewels from the collar ornament."

I shook my head. "I thought Sean told you not to talk to the police. Did Marsha tell them about your deal?"

"Absolutely not," Pris said with a vehement shake of her head. She pulled the rubber gloves on and squared off against Jinx, who still sat content in the sink. "Like I said, Marsha's a perfectly lovely woman. It was my oaf of a husband. Hal keeps secrets all the time, but *this* time, when it was my behind on the line, he sang like a freakin' lark. So helpful."

Pris had confided in me long ago that her marriage with Hal was a sham. They'd long since lost interest in each other, and half the town knew that Hal had had affairs with anyone he could get his hands on— from members of the Methodist Ladies' Auxiliary to strippers from a trucker joint a few counties over. The problem was a prenuptial agreement. Pris walked away with very little if she started divorce proceedings. She had two outs. First, if Hal filed the papers, it would break the agreement, but Hal was happily holding on to his cake while eating it, too; he had no incentive to file for divorce and risk his fortune. The second out was if Pris had proof of Hal's infidelity. His skirt chasing was one of the most poorly kept secrets in Merryville, but it remained undocumented.

I wondered if there was some clause in that agreement about what would happen if Pris went to prison. Either way, Hal had no real reason to be loyal to his wife and try to protect her good name, especially if protecting her meant her problem cast shade on his own ambitions.

"But there's no way you would have known that killing Phillip would resolve your business problems."

She laughed. "If you could just convince your boyfriend of that fact, I'd be in good shape. Now, let me get down to work and wash this cat."

At that point, the water came on and the claws came out. I just stood back and watched the fun. I watched as Pris expertly held Jinx in place, foreclosing the opportunity to leap out of the tub or even to gain some leverage against the tub's sides. Jinx swatted at Pris, but the gloves Pris wore rendered Jinx's claws useless.

When Pris turned on the sprayer to get Jinx's head wet, my cat turned a baleful eye on me.

J'accuse.

I had to look away from the combination of anger and fear in Jinx's eyes. We had a pact, she and I. I could dress her up without being clawed to ribbons so long as we didn't use the tub. I felt a pang of remorse that I was putting poor Jinx through this just to enter her in the pageant. After all, the show cats had been raised being handled and bathed, so they didn't mind it, but Jinx was another story.

She let out a full-throated cry, and I came *this* close to snatching her out of her bath right then and there. But unforgiving, brittle, cold Pris Olson did the most amazing thing. She cooed softly to my cat and applied pressure to some magic place on the back of her neck so she calmed down.

Jinx settled in for the rest of the bath, not putting

up any fuss at all—even when Pris set her in the dryer box—but she continued to give me the hairy eyeball. No doubt about it. Sometime, someplace where I least expected it, Jinx would get me back for this indignity. We'd had an understanding, and I'd broken it . . . and I was going to pay.

CHAPTER
Seventeen

I had hemmed and hawed about entering Jinx in the household-pet division of the cat show, but in the end I was glad I did it.

After Pris had finished shampooing and fluffing and combing my beautiful girl, I combed through Jinxie's fur some fuller's earth I'd borrowed from Ruth before she passed. The fuller's earth did what Ducky White had done for Ruth's Ranger by absorbing extra oil in Jinx's coat, but it didn't have the same whitening properties. By the time I was done, my Jinx looked nearly twice her usual gigantic size.

I brought her—stripped naked—from her large kennel on the Trendy Tails table to the judging ring in her normal-sized cat carrier and then stood back as the clerk for the ring placed her in one of the wire holding pens. The process of unloading the cats into their pens for judging took longer than I expected. Apparently, it was critical to get the right cat in the right pen. Even though household pets could only compete if they were spayed or neutered, there was still a policy of keeping the boys separated by at least one pen so they didn't get into turf wars with one another.

Finally, I stood back and watched the judging.

At first I was terrified that Jinx would do something to get us both thrown out, but the very first cat up for judging, a lithe black cat that looked like she had some Siamese in her, piddled on the judging table. The judge, an older woman who wore her glasses on a chain around her neck, chuckled good-naturedly and continued to hold the cat while the clerk scurried in to clean up the mess. I was pretty sure that Jinx wasn't going to do anything more inappropriate than that.

And she didn't. In fact, my girl was a perfect little lady.

"Who's this big girl?" the judge asked when the clerk brought her to the table.

"That's Jinx," I called back from the circle of onlookers.

"Well, hello, Jinx. Aren't you a fine cat? Looks like Jinx has a good amount of Norwegian forest cat in her, though she might have a little Maine coon, too. Certainly from the big breeds, that's for sure. Nice color." The judge ran her hands down Jinx's side. "Mmm-hmm. Good body type, but Mama out there might want to go a little easier on the kibble. Miss Jinx is carrying a few extra pounds."

While her words should perhaps have embarrassed me, I found myself laughing along with the rest of the small crowd.

When she picked Jinx up to display her Uzi-style to the crowd, I held my breath. If Jinx was going to pitch a fit, this was when she'd do it. But my good girl just hung limp in the judge's hands.

She got a big round of applause, and I swear I saw a little sparkle in her eye when the judge set her down and ruffled her ears playfully.

"You did not see a sparkle in her eye," Rena said when we got back to the table. "Now you're going to be like one of those pageant moms who says their three-month-old loves to compete."

"I am not."

"You absolutely are. You're saying Jinx actually enjoyed being shown off in front of all those people."

"Fine. Maybe she didn't enjoy it, but she didn't hate it."

I was in the process of pulling Jinx's apparel du jour—a hot-pink hoodie with a faux-fur-trimmed hood—back onto her body, when T. J. Leuzinger wandered up to the table.

"I hear you took second place in household."

I felt like my kid had just won the spelling bee. "Yes. Jinx here did the hard part."

"Right," Rena said. "The hard part of being beautiful."

T.J. grinned and patted her own teased-out hair. "Being beautiful isn't exactly a walk in the park."

Rena and I laughed. T.J. was a whole lot of personality, but she was growing on me.

"Have you given any more thought to what Ruth might have meant the other day about it being in the blood?" I asked.

"It haunts me. It truly does. But I just don't know what she was talking about."

"We were thinking that she might have meant something to do with breeding."

"Ah." T.J. nodded sagely. "The whole Pamela Rawlins fiasco. Could be. But why would she have suddenly wanted to tell you about that? You already knew about the breeding scandal. What could Ruth have seen on her trip up to her room that made her so urgent to talk to you?"

At least the connection to Pamela came naturally to T.J. I had thought maybe I was forcing a round peg into a square hole, but when T.J. thought "breeding," she thought of Pamela and Tonga, too.

I lifted a shoulder in response to T.J.'s question, and suddenly my limp cat became as stiff as a board in my hands, using her back feet to launch off my body and out into the mayhem of the show.

T.J. and Rena both looked at me with eyes as big and as round as moonflowers. I had just committed the cardinal sin of cat shows: I'd lost control of my animal.

I dashed into the fray, searching for Jinx, hoping to find her before she got stepped on or got into a scuffle with another cat. I'd never known her to put up a fuss around other animals, even at the parties we'd held at Trendy Tails, but she'd never been loose in such a raucous environment. I had no idea how she would react.

"Jinx," I hissed, as though she might hear me above the din of nearly five hundred people all talking simultaneously.

T.J., who was helping me, crossed from one row to the next ahead of me, and so I skipped a row and began sweeping down a new line of tables. I was walking bent at the waist and didn't see trouble coming until I barreled into it.

Pamela Rawlins.

As always, she stood straight as a birch, her pale body encased in somber black clothes. She wore her hair up, exposing the long expanse of her neck, and were it not for the carnelian lipstick she wore and the gold locket around her neck, she could have passed for a corpse.

"Ms. McHale? What on earth are you doing?"

"Nothing," I replied too quickly. Over Pamela's shoulder, I caught sight of T.J., and our gazes latched for a second. As soon as she saw whom I was talking to, she dashed away.

"You'll forgive me if I have a hard time swallowing that. I've heard from my sources that you've been carrying on your own private investigation of our unfortunate events. I'd ask you to leave those matters to the police."

I stood straight and met her eyes. "Why?" I asked boldly. My promise to Sean had vanished like morning fog. "Are you worried I might find something?"

"Of all the rude . . . Of course not. Why would I have anything to hide?"

"Well, Phillip did ruin your breeding business by banning Tonga from shows."

"That's true," Pamela conceded, "but that turns out to have been a blessing in disguise. When the breeding contracts started drying up, I began looking for another way to supplement my alimony income. I'd always been a quilter, but lately I've been doing it in earnest. Selling my goods on Peter Denford's site, theartisanway.com. I've been making money like I never dreamed was possible."

I felt something brush my leg and resisted the urge to look down. If it was Jinx, I could hardly scoop her up right in front of Pamela Rawlins.

"So you're telling me that you suddenly have no interest in showing cats?"

"Of course not. I still have Tonga, and I'll probably buy another show cat once my quilting business stabilizes, but right now I'm content with what I've done."

It didn't seem possible that the woman who had fought so hard to coordinate the M-CFO silver anniversary could be so cavalier about leaving the world of cat shows. "What about planning the shows?" I asked. "You've been so adamant about being in charge of this, yet Phillip's ill will meant you weren't going to be able to plan next year's show."

She laughed. "If my goal was to keep my finger in the show, killing Phillip was really the wrong way to go about it. It's true Phillip and I weren't on the best of terms, and he was planning on cutting me from the planning committee in the future, but at least he had some soft spot for me."

To the extent you can blackmail someone into a soft spot, I thought.

"With Phillip dead, Marsha is in charge. And, if you haven't noticed, the two of us don't really get along. If I were interested, Marsha would give me the boot for certain. But I'm not. One of the other wonderful changes that has come my way because of my shift in focus to quilting is that I've met a wonderful man. He lives in Dallas, and I'm going to be moving down this winter to be with him. When I rejoin the cat-show circuit, and I do anticipate doing so someday, I won't be part of the Midwest region. My interest in the M-CFO ends with this show."

I decided I had little to lose. Pamela seemed to be in a talkative mood, so I pushed my luck. Pamela might have a new love interest, but from the way Mari had acted around Jack, she was very, very single. I wanted to learn what I could about the romantic entanglements in this group, and now that she didn't have any skin in the game, I thought maybe I'd get Pamela to talk about her relationship with Phillip.

"The animosity between you and Marsha Denford is hard to miss. Is that because of your affair with Phillip Denford?"

"What?" She threw back her head and howled. "Oh dear. Ms. McHale. How little you know." She let her laughter run its course, while I stood there, feeling like an idiot and the rest of the cat fanciers looked on in curiosity.

"No, no, no," she said when she'd regained her composure. "First, I admit to a little fling with Phillip, but it was more than a year ago and strictly utilitarian. Second, Marsha is well aware of Phillip's infidelities and is, I think, almost grateful for them. Phillip is— was—a rich and powerful man, but hardly worth squabbling over. I harbor no illusions that Phillip and I were a love match, and if he ever decided to trade in Marsha, it would have been for a newer model . . . not an older woman. If Marsha had any real competition for Phillip's affections, it was from Mari. That child is young both physically and emotionally. Right up Phillip's alley."

"Do you think Mari and Phillip were that serious?"

Pamela pursed her lips in thought. "No. Something tells me that Mari was simply convenient for Phillip. Lord knows, he never shows anything but contempt for her in public. Maybe things are different in private, but I have a hard time imagining that. I think Marsha's role as Mrs. Denford was safe."

"So if you weren't fighting over Phillip, what's the beef between you and Marsha about?"

"From my end, I have no patience with her loopy personality. I come from a line of straight-talking women." This did not surprise me. "It's in my blood to distrust people who won't give you a straight answer when you ask for one. From her side, maybe she's just reacting to my impatience. Or, I suppose . . ."

"You suppose what?"

"Well, I've been spending a lot of time with Peter lately, providing input on the launch of theartisanway.com. Peter and Marsha are quite close. She may be angry that I'm monopolizing so much of his time."

"Sounds like she's quite a clingy mother."

Pamela laughed, a low, throaty sound. "Mother? Peter didn't even meet Marsha until he was a grown man. They've just become so close because they both live in the frigid shadow of Phillip Denford." She brushed a piece of imaginary lint from her sleeve. "Now, if you'll excuse me, I still have a closing ceremony to put on tonight. I hope I'll see you at the masquerade."

With that, she melted back into the crowd.

I immediately dropped to my knees to look around for Jinx, but still saw no sign of her. When I stood, I saw a flash of movement out of the corner of my eye and turned to see Rena, my diminutive friend, jumping up and down and waving her arms to snag my attention.

I hustled my bustle muscle back to the Trendy Tails station, hoping that she'd found Jinx. It seemed, instead, that Jinx had found her.

My big fluffy cat sat smack in the middle of the aisle, as calm as she could be, holding Gandhi the guinea pig by the scruff of his neck, just like a mama cat would with a wayward kitten.

CHAPTER
Eighteen

We managed to get Gandhi away from Jinx with a minimum of growling and absolutely no bloodshed. Jinx went in her big showcase kennel, clothed to model a pair of cat's pajamas, and Gandhi got shoved in Jinx's smaller kennel for transport home.

It felt good to hear the clink of the metal kennel latches and to see Gandhi crouched down in the carrier. Gandhi had left human care about nine months earlier. He'd fared well, considering he'd survived a Minnesota winter on his own, but his free roaming days had taken their toll. He wasn't as plump as he'd been when Sherry Harper had carried him around in a baby sling, and his lovely auburn tufts had grown matted. I wouldn't feel comfortable until he got an all clear from the vet, but he looked like he'd survived and would live to burrow another day.

Mari Aames stormed up to our table. "Izzy McHale, I should be reading you the riot act for letting your cat get out of your control, but it seems that Jinx here saved the day. Who knows what kind of damage might have been done if the other cats caught the scent of that rodent? I'm going to file a complaint with the hotel about this near fiasco."

I held up a hand in protest. "No! Please don't do that. I actually know this guinea pig."

Mari looked puzzled. "He's an acquaintance of yours?"

"Yes. His name is Gandhi." I proceeded to regale Mari with the saga of Gandhi and our inability to catch the wily critter. By the time I was done, Mari was tearing up.

"Poor little guy," she muttered. This, to an animal she might have roasted on a spit not ten minutes earlier.

"I promise I'll take him home as soon as there's a break in the action. Soon."

"Okay. I guess we can just let it slide. It's actually nice to have a happy ending around here."

"I know this whole event must have been very difficult for you, Mari," Rena said. "I get the sense you were very close with Mr. Denford."

For an instant, Mari looked panicked, but then her

face fell again. I was starting to get used to tragic Mari.

"We were. I was a dedicated employee."

Hmmm. No mention of what kind of employer Phillip had been. Something told me the dedication didn't run in both directions.

"What's that smell?" Mari said.

"I don't smell anything other than cat," Rena replied.

"No. There's something . . . sweet." She clutched her hands over her mouth and scooted away with a mumbled apology.

"That was weird," I said.

"Nah. She's just preggers."

I looked at Rena like she'd sprouted horns. "How can you possibly know that?"

"Well, part of it is my special gift. You know how some dogs can tell if their owner is about to have a seizure? I can tell when people are pregnant. And Mari's pregnant."

I cuffed her shoulder. "That's a pretty bold statement to make on a hunch."

Rena rolled her eyes. "It's not *just* a hunch. The crazy mood swings, hypersensitivity to smells, regular puking . . ."

How could I not have noticed? That explained, too, why Mari had been so reluctant to drink her prosecco at lunch at the Red, White & Bleu.

"This makes perfect sense," I said. "If Mari was in love with Phillip and having his baby, but he was planning to fire her, as T.J. said he was, Mari had plenty of reason to be furious with the man. We've all been assuming that the murder was premeditated, but what if it wasn't? Someone was driving Phillip around the morning he was murdered, and that was probably his assistant. They get back to the ballroom, he says something mean or snarky to her, and she grabs the pair of grooming shears from Ruth's table and stabs him."

Rena nodded. "Yeah, that does make sense. Though it doesn't explain the theft of the collar dangle."

"If Mari knew she was having a baby and was losing her income, maybe she saw the dangle as her baby's birthright."

"Birthright? What century are you living in? She didn't need a birthright; she needed state-mandated child support."

"Okay, fair enough. Mari's pregnancy doesn't explain the theft, but it really does fit the murder scenario to a tee. T.J. said Ruth and Mari left the ballroom at about the same time, and Mari looked like she was sick. If Ruth encountered Mari in a moment of weakness, Mari might have spilled the whole story. And that would explain Ruth's cryptic comment about 'it' being in the blood."

Rena narrowed her eyes and bent to straighten a

stack of delicate ruffs—simple elasticized circles of satin and embroidered fabric that could be slipped around the cat's neck. "I'll admit, it's a pretty compelling story. But I'm not entirely sold."

I sighed. "Me neither. But it's worth investigating a little further."

I was at a stoplight on the way home when I got a text from Ama Olmstead asking me to join her at her apartment. I couldn't leave Gandhi in the car, and showing up with a rodent in tow seemed rude, so I swung by Trendy Tails to drop off the guinea pig—careful to set his carrier high enough that Packer couldn't mess with him—before heading to Ama's house.

When Ama and I had first gotten to know each other, she'd been living with her husband in a lovely little house with an office for her in a converted mother-in-law apartment. But after her separation from her husband, she'd moved into a smaller one-and-a-half-story cottage with stucco walls and whimsical wrought iron framing a wide front door.

When you entered, it appeared that most of the house was consumed by a large living room with coved ceilings and a massive fireplace. A small dining area lay beyond the living room, a kitchen and two small bedrooms tucked behind it.

I followed Ama up the stairs to the expansion space with its gabled ceilings and open-floor plan. Oddly, the new house was smaller than the old, but the size of Ama's office had actually grown.

She directed me to a rolling chair next to the desk. As she sat down, she snapped a piece of nicotine gum from its blister pack and popped it in her mouth.

"You've given up smoking?"

"I'm trying," she said. "The last few months have had me reevaluating a number of my life choices."

"Good for you!"

"So here's what I have," she said. We sat before a giant monitor covered with a grid of thumbnails of photos from the day of the show opening. She began flipping through them one at a time.

"You were right. I don't have a picture with Pris in it right before the blackout. Ordinarily, that wouldn't mean much. There were a ton of people there, so I could have easily missed her. But here's the interesting thing."

She clicked on a thumbnail, and it expanded to fill about half the screen. "This is one of the first pictures I took that day, right as the doors were opening at nine. I wanted to get a couple of shots of the people thronging into the ballroom, so I stood right near your table and took a couple of shots toward the main door and then over the heads of the crowd, with my camera pointed right toward the other front corner, where Pris's booth was."

Right there, in the background but clear as day,

was Pris. "Just like Rena said. She was there when the doors opened."

"And check out what she's wearing."

In the picture, Pris wore a dark suit coat and a red shell. Because of the crowd, I couldn't tell whether she was wearing pants or a skirt, but she was definitely in a suit.

"Now we flip forward," she said as she slid her mouse along the desk, causing each picture to pop up in turn. "This is the last picture I got before the lights went out. Hands down the best. The cropped version went on the front page of the *Gazette*."

I recognized the image from my evening at the police department. It was, indeed, a great picture. In the original photo, though, the framing was wider, a bit less artsy, and you could see a handful of people clustered near the prize table. Three whom I recognized: Ruth Kimmey, Peter Denford, and Mari Aames.

Ama continued to breeze through the postblackout shots, and I caught glimpses of crime-scene tape, a shot of Jack directing someone to move, and a couple photos of crime-scene investigators removing Phillip's body. Finally, after dozens of frames, she stopped.

"And then I happened to catch this." It was a picture taken from farther back in the ballroom. In the foreground you could see me talking with Pamela, Mari, and Marsha. In the background I could just see the door behind Pris's grooming booth, with none other than Pris herself coming through the door.

"So she *was* gone when the collar dangle was stolen."

"I don't know about gone, but definitely not in the room. The interesting thing, though, is that she'd changed."

"What?"

I looked more closely. Sure enough, Pris was no longer wearing the dark suit. She was wearing a blush-colored sleeveless top and a pair of pale slacks. The look was definitely more casual than what she had been wearing before.

Was it possible? Had Pris killed Phillip and waited around in bloodstained clothes until there were people in the ballroom and *then* gone off to change? It hadn't occurred to me as a possibility, because in my head Pris was wearing her usual shades of pale pink, pale blue, and white, colors on which she couldn't have hidden so much as a drop of blood from anyone. But if she'd been dressed in dark colors that morning, she could have hidden a smattering of blood for a bit during the crush of the opening of the show. It was possible, but was that what had really happened? And if Pris had killed Phillip, had she also lingered long enough to throw the fuses and sneak in to steal the dangle under cover of darkness?

Something didn't seem right.

I still wasn't sure what had happened the morning

Phillip died, but I knew my next stop had to be to talk to Pris again.

I found her where I'd left her, at Prissy's Pretty Pets.

She was no longer alone, though. Dee Dee Lahti had apparently returned from the cat show to pick up some additional supplies.

Dee Dee didn't have the good sense God gave itty-bitty bunnies. Whatever sense of dignity she'd ever had had been beaten out of her by her husband, a man who casually slipped in and out of criminal activity. Still, Dee Dee had one joy in her life: her dog, Pumpkin. She'd taken on the position of gofer for Pris's shop so that she could occasionally get the tiny Shih Tzu groomed. I'd given her a few outfits for the dog, always careful to point out that they were prototypes, items I couldn't sell, so she wouldn't think the gifts were charity. Taffy did the same thing with her day-old baked goods. "Please take them. You'd be doing me such a favor."

In short, the women of Merryville rallied around Dee Dee. We couldn't protect her from her no-good husband—only Dee Dee herself could do that with a call to the Merryville PD—but we could make the rest of her life a little easier

When I arrived at Prissy's Pretty Pets, Dee Dee was loading a plastic tub with towels and a few bottles of shampoo. Her purple muumuu swished around her as she gathered up the items in an apparent frenzy, but she came to a screeching halt when she saw me.

"Izzy!" She shuffled over and gave me a hug that smelled of menthols and mothballs. "I haven't had a chance to talk to you in a long time."

"I know. We've both been on the floor of that cat show for days, but there's hardly time to think, let alone talk."

"Are you enjoying the show?"

"As much as possible, under the circumstances."

Dee Dee nodded solemnly. "Yes, Mr. Denford's murder was very sad. Ms. Marsha doesn't let people see, but I've caught her crying three times now. Our booth is relatively quiet, so she just comes back and sits there."

I couldn't imagine how Marsha was holding up as well as she was. Well, actually, I could. The occasional Xanax did wonders for keeping tears in check.

Still, the pain of losing her husband must have been so raw. Granted, her husband was a good twenty years older than she was, chased skirts like a champ, and was overall a not very nice man. But in the end he was still her husband, and the loss of that intimacy and stability was dreadful. I'd had a small taste of that feeling when my boyfriend of seventeen years dumped me, but if I really wanted to, I could call Casey, hear his voice, remember the good times in our relationship. Marsha didn't have that option.

Pris emerged from the back of the store. "Dee Dee, you need to hustle those things over to the cat show. Mandy just called in a panic because they have only one towel left."

"Sorry," Dee Dee muttered. She picked up her basket of goodies and headed to the back of the shop, where I was sure there was an alley entrance.

Pris shook her head. "That one is a piece of work."

I couldn't hold back a smile. "She sure is. But it seems like things are working out okay with her working here at the store."

Pris waggled a hand. "So-so. She's great with the animals, but she doesn't have the patience or the attention span to actually finish any project she starts. The other girls hate working with her because they say they spend all their time cleaning up after her."

"Would you let her go?"

"No," Pris said adamantly. "Those girls need to learn to overcome obstacles and troubleshoot. I like to think of Dee Dee as a walking, talking life lesson." She sighed. "There but for the grace of God and good genes . . .

"Now," she said, voice crisp and businesslike. "What brings you back so soon? Was there a problem with Jinx?"

"Not at all," I assured her. "I just had a question for you."

"And the phone wouldn't do?"

"Nope. Serious question."

Pris sighed. We had been getting along better since we'd started working on the cat show together, but I still knew that Pris barely tolerated me and my small-town outlook on life.

"The morning of Phillip Denford's murder, why did you change clothes?"

"Excuse me?"

"I just got back from Ama Olmstead's house. She has tons of pictures from that morning. When the show opened, you were wearing a black suit. Then you were MIA for a while, and then you made it into a picture just after the blackout, but you were dressed in a pale pair of slacks and a more casual tunic top."

"What does my wardrobe have to do with anything?"

"If you were wearing a black suit when Phillip was murdered, it would have hid the bloodstains until you had a chance to go change. And you were clearly gone at the beginning of the blackout, yet you told the police you were present in the ballroom and talking to Ruth Kimmey. Why would you lie about that if you didn't have something to hide? And why change your clothes at all unless the black suit had to be dumped?"

Pris motioned me to two hot-pink velvet chairs in the waiting area of the shop. I took a seat and so did Pris.

"I thought you were on my side," Pris said.

"I'm on the side of figuring out the truth," I replied.

"I still think the crime seems a little too . . . messy for your taste, but the photographic evidence is damning."

"Why not take this straight to your boyfriend?"

It was a fair question. I could have easily turned the information over to him or taken it straight to Gil Dixon, who was heading up the investigation. Let the pros figure it out.

"For some reason, I really want to believe in you, Pris. I've had too many instances in my life when I've misjudged someone's character and it's had serious repercussions . . . trusting people who turned out to be cheats and liars and worse. I don't want to be wrong about you. And I don't want to give more fodder to the police to use against you if you really are innocent."

"You do realize we're not friends."

"Of course. But we've got our bonds, however tenuous they may be, and I don't want to break them."

Pris leaned back in the pink wingback, closed her eyes, and took a few deep breaths.

"Here's why you're wrong, Izzy. First of all, the notion that a dark suit would hide the blood from Phillip's murder is ridiculous. The man was stabbed in the neck with a pair of shears. There would have been blood everywhere. I don't think I could have confined the blood spray to my suit without getting it on my body and in my hair."

"But there wasn't any blood at all—or, at least, not enough to notice—in the space behind the prize table where Phillip would have been standing when he was murdered. The way he was stabbed must have caused him to bleed out more slowly."

Pris rolled her eyes. "Okay, fine. Let's say that I really could have managed to keep blood hidden on a black pantsuit while I greeted cat show goers and directed my girls in opening the grooming station. Let's assume that none of them would have noticed the darker wet patches. I had a perfectly normal reason for changing my clothes."

"And what is that?"

"The suit wasn't appropriate for the cat show. Pamela Rawlins may traipse around in her all-black wardrobe, but it's summer. It's time to wear lighter, fresher colors and something a little more casual and appropriate for the day."

"So why put on the suit in the first place?"

Here she gave real pause. I could see the wheels turning behind her cerulean eyes.

"This is between us, right? You're not wearing a wire while Jack Collins waits in the car? You're not recording this conversation?"

"Yes, no, and no. Whatever you tell me stays between us . . . unless you incriminate yourself."

"Fair. I, uh, had an errand to run that morning."

"And you needed to wear a suit? What kind of errand?"

"I went to see a lawyer. A divorce lawyer."

Pris had told me before that her relationship with Hal was a sham, that she wanted out but only if she could take half his money with her. She'd put up with a lot from the man and felt she deserved her share of their wealth. But given a rigid prenup, the only way that would happen was if she got proof of Hal cheating.

"Did you get pictures of Hal with another woman?"

Pris laughed. "I wish. No, it's just that I've been holding out for half of Hal's fortune. With the fortune gone, half of nothing is nothing. I figured I might as well make an escape. So I got dressed up to meet the lawyer, then changed into more cat-show-appropriate clothes when I got back."

"But why hide this from the police?"

"Because, like I said, with Phillip's death and the Department of Natural Resources on the brink of ruling in our favor, our future earning potential was looking up. Now it's worth biding my time, seeing if Hal can fix his finances and get us back to the standard of living I've grown accustomed to."

"But still. Tell the police. Just because people know you saw a lawyer doesn't mean you have to go through with the divorce." I leaned forward in my chair, willing

Pris to see that her lie was unnecessary and if Ama took her information to the police—or, worse, the press—Pris could be ruined.

"You don't understand, Izzy. If Hal divorces me, I get nothing."

"But why would he divorce you? You've been together for years."

"Hal has political ambitions. The position of mayor is just the first step in what Hal hopes will be a long and successful political career. But he knows what people think of him. He's got this good-ol'-boy image that might work in Merryville but would be a tough sell for statewide office. I'm his polish. That's why he's kept me all these years."

"So, you're still his polish."

"Not if I go to a lawyer. Then, suddenly, I become a chink in his armor. I become the marital problem that will haunt his campaigns. I become an embarrassment. At that point, he's just as good without me as he is with me. As long as there's still hope for a financial windfall, I can't have Hal dumping me."

CHAPTER
Nineteen

I was blessed with some of the best friends a girl could hope to have, but sometimes that girl just needs her mom.

My parents still live in the house in which I grew up, still host dinners every Sunday afternoon to bring us all together, so I'm truly going home when I visit them.

The living room hadn't changed a whit since I was a child. My parents were comfortable, but too frugal to go buy new furniture just because the plaid sofa and burnt-umber chairs were no longer fashionable. I sat in the corner of the sofa that had always been mine and pulled a needlepoint throw pillow up to my chest.

My dad, a tall man with hair the color of frost,

came over to ruffle my hair and kiss my forehead. Then he slipped through the pocket doors that led to his study, pulled out one of his beloved history books, and kicked back his recliner.

My parents had both taught at Merryville High, Mom, English and Dad, history and geography. Retired now, they each continued their passion in life. Where my mother focused her energies outward, continuing to tutor adults for their GED exams and assisting the community theater with their productions of classic plays, my dad had drifted farther and farther into himself. He seemed to delight in the stories we told over Sunday dinner, but he kept to himself. We all knew he continued to love us dearly, but he'd long since realized that the problems of daughters are often best managed by mothers. So he didn't even question why I'd shown up on a random afternoon; he just kissed me and disappeared.

"So what's going on, Izzy?"

"I just wanted to see you."

My mother cocked her head. "That's lovely, dear, but with all you have going on, 'just seeing me' could have waited until Sunday. Tell me what's really going on."

"Would you be willing to take on a guinea pig?"

"Well, that's certainly not what I was expecting."

"It's Gandhi. We've finally captured him, but I don't know what to do with him. Rena can't take him home because Val would try to eat him. I have the same problem with Jinx. I'm just not sure where he can go and be safe."

My mom smiled. "Tell you what. You can bring him over here for a few weeks and then, just before school starts, you can find an elementary school class in need of a guinea pig. Fair?"

"Fair? That's brilliant. I never would have thought of taking him to a school, but it's genius."

"Now, my precious girl, tell my why you're *really* here. That guinea pig makes a great excuse for you to drop in, but I can tell you're troubled."

I stared into the middle distance for a few moments, allowing the silence to build between us. When I spoke, my voice didn't sound like my own.

"I think I just needed to be reminded that real love and honest marriages do still exist. I just talked to Pris, and you know what a sham her marriage to Hal is. And I've been talking with everyone about the Denfords, and it seems their marriage was even worse. While Hal at least attempts to keep his shenanigans a secret, Phillip Denford was having an affair with his secretary right under his wife's nose. And while Pris is a little low on friends at the moment, she does enjoy ruling the women of Merryville with her mighty will. From what I can discern, poor Marsha is left with no support, save her stepson and several prescriptions for numbness."

I sighed. "And then there's my own life, with Casey claiming to love me for all those years only to leave me when our dreams were about to come to fruition."

"Well, I can't speak for the Olsons or the Denfords, but you did make a mighty mistake trusting that Casey Alter."

I clutched my pillow tighter and stared at my mom. She was a trim woman, much shorter than her girls, with a halo of salt-and-pepper curls and expressive amber eyes. In her day, she'd been a babe, and she was aging well.

"Mom, how can you say that? It's not like I could have known that Casey was going to dump me."

My mother leaned back in the oversized armchair she favored. "I don't see why not. All the rest of us could see it coming a mile away."

"Well, for the love of Mike, why didn't one of you tell me? Prepare me for the heartache?" If I'd come looking for tea and sympathy, I'd come to the wrong woman. My sister Dru came by her straight-talking honestly, a clear mimic of my mother.

"I would have done anything to spare you that misery, but telling you wouldn't have done a lick of good. You were in love, and if one of us had said something ill about your beloved, it would have caused a rift in the family. Besides, your father and I have always believed it was best to let you girls make your own mistakes and learn the lessons from them."

I rolled my eyes. "What lesson did I learn from wasting seventeen years of my life? The whole thing seems to have made me afraid of any sort of commitment."

"Not true. You and Casey were both caught up in the life you had planned together. I'm not saying you didn't love him, but at least part of your feelings stemmed from your dreams of the future. You were always talking about how great your life would be when you moved to New York, like the city was some magic drug that would fix all your problems. What I *hope* you learned is that real love is in the here and now. You have to love someone for who he is, not who he'll become."

I twined a lock of hair around one finger and thought about what she'd said. It was true that Casey and I'd had every step of our lives planned out, and I was in love with our destination. I put up with a lot of crap from him because I thought it would all get better.

"Mom, I'm afraid he broke my heart too bad."

My mother left her chair to come sit by me and wrap her arms around me. "Baby, you have the biggest heart I know. Casey may have rattled it, but it's not broken. Look at how close you've grown to Jack."

I pressed my cheek to her sweater. "That's just it. I

love Jack, but I'm having a hard time committing to the relationship. I just don't quite feel like I'm all in, you know?"

Mom pulled away and brushed the hair from my eyes so she could look into them. "People always say that love is fast and exciting in the beginning and then the fun fades. But that's not true. Love is like a roller coaster. There is a thrilling rush of anticipation as you climb that first big hill, but then, for a moment, you're teetering at the top and you think, 'Wow, this was a terrible idea.' The biggest rush is when you let yourself fall over the other side. That's where you are now, darling girl. You're at that magical terrifying height, and all you have to do is let yourself fall."

"Are you saying I'm overthinking things?"

My mother laughed. "Absolutely. But it's not your fault. It's in your blood. Look at how Dru dithers over every decision, and Lucy is going to lead that Xander on a merry chase before he gets her to settle down. And I have to admit, I made your father propose three times before I got the courage to say yes."

"You're right," I mumbled. "It's in my blood."

That's what Ruth Kimmey had been trying to tell me before she died. *It's in the blood.* It had nothing to do with cat breeding and everything to do with people breeding. The only blood relatives I knew from the cat show were Peter and Phillip Denford. Was Ruth trying to tell me that the son had more in common with the father than it appeared? If so, what could the connection be?

"Mom, you've been a huge help."

"Aren't I always?"

I wrapped my arms around her and hugged her back before standing to go. "You're always a help, but today even more than usual. And, for what it's worth, I'll let myself fall. I promise."

The night of the masquerade ball that would close the M-CFO Silver Anniversary Retreat, Rena and I were working at Trendy Tails, trying to figure out how much we'd made at the show. The numbers looked good, and I went to get a bottle of wine for a quick celebratory toast before we had to start getting ready for the ball.

When I returned from the kitchen, glasses and bottle in hand, Rena was just putting her phone in her pocket. "That was Shane at the Silent Woman, letting me know that I need to come pick up my dad."

"Really? It's only six."

"Dad's drunk doesn't really have a schedule. I can do this alone," she insisted. "Lucy and Dru will be here any minute, and I don't want to spoil the fun of getting dressed up for you all."

"I know you can handle it, but I'd feel better if I came with you to make sure everything goes down okay. If there's a herd of bikers moving through town, the Woman can get a little rowdy. Just let me do this for you. Besides, it won't be any fun getting ready without you there with us."

We took Rena's car, a hoopty Korean compact whose odometer had given up counting the miles long ago, when it rolled over 124K, and drove out of the historic district and into Merryville's light industrial center.

The Silent Woman smelled of rancid beer, ammonia, and despair. It was located, quite literally, on the wrong side of the tracks: it backed up to the railroad tracks that ran along Merryville's south side. While it's not the sort of establishment I frequent, I'd been to the bar several times in my day, primarily on the same mission I was on today: bailing out Rena's dad when he'd outstayed his welcome.

That's right. Outstayed his welcome. It's an impressive feat to be so drunk that even the Silent Woman wants to oust you. Normally, they let people stay as long as they paid their tabs. Fall asleep? No problem; you weren't hurting anything. Start singing at the top of your lungs? Not great, but the injury was aesthetic, no more than skin-deep. But Bruce Hamilton went through stages of drunk the way other people go through stages of grief, and some of them weren't pretty. Take a swing at a bartender? That got you thrown out of the bar and possibly thrown into the drunk tank.

In fact, if Bruce weren't such a good customer, he'd probably be in custody instead of facing off against his waif of a daughter, debating how, when, and why he would leave.

The temptation to weigh in to their conversation was strong, but I'd learned long ago that it was a mistake to mess with the volatile dynamic between father and daughter.

"Can I buy you a drink, pretty lady?"

The man sat at the bar, jeans riding low so that he was sitting on the waistband, a loose black hoodie hanging from his shoulders. Oily strands of dark hair fell across a face that was almost handsome. I couldn't pinpoint what was off—the set of his eyes, the shape of his nose, the gap above his upper lip—but something made him look vaguely troll-like. He clasped a glass of beer like he was warming his hands by it.

"I think I'll pass. But thank you."

"You're a tall drink of water," he continued.

"Thank you?"

"Aw, that's definitely a compliment. I like tall women. You're maybe even taller than me, but that's okay."

"I have a boyfriend," I blurted.

He threw back his head and cackled. "I got a woman, too. Doesn't mean we can't conversate a little over a couple of beers."

"Leave her alone, Jonnie." Rena moved to stand between us, as though she would protect me from this creep. I had no doubt that Rena was tougher than I was and she knew how to fight dirty, but I outweighed her by a good forty pounds. I loved that she still felt the need to play the part of guard dog.

"You ready to leave?" I asked.

"Nah." Rena sighed. "Dad's not budging. It's going to be a police kind of night. I promised Shane"—the owner of the bar—"that I would stick around until they get Dad packed off to the PD. He won't come with me, but he won't put up as much of a fuss with the cops if I'm around."

Rena's dad was a longtime alcoholic. His drinking predated his wife's death, but when Rena's mom died during Rena's junior year in high school, her dad went off the rails. Rena had been taking care of him ever since, and taking care of him often meant negotiating the best way to get him to a safe spot to sober up.

"Well, if you're waiting for the cops, you have to have a drink with me. Can't just stand there, right?"

"Since we're waiting for the cops," Rena said to Jonnie, "you might want to boogie."

"Why?" I asked, studying my suitor with narrowed eyes.

"Izzy, meet Jonnie G. Merryville's most active fence."

"Come on," Jonnie protested. "I do faxilitate the sale of goods from one person to another, and like any businessman, I take a small cut of those transactions.

But I'm not a fence. Near as I know, all those transactions are perfectly legalistic."

"Just because you don't ask the questions doesn't mean you don't know the answers. You're a fence."

Jonnie chuckled. "Don't go libeling my good name in front of your foxy friend, Rena. Not cool."

They nattered back and forth the way I'd traded insults with my sisters when we were younger, poking at sore spots but with no real sense of malice. I half listened to them while the wheels in my mind were turning.

"Uh, Jonnie. What kind of goods do you help people sell?"

"Why? You have something to unload?"

"No. I was just wondering if you helped people sell jewelry."

"Occasionally. More often I transact in electronics and, uh, construction materials, but I've been known to find buyers for the occasional trinket."

"You ever do anything like that for Pris Olson?"

Rena tilted forward on her toes, as anxious for the answer as I was.

Jonnie pursed his lips and considered me thoughtfully. "I'm not sure it is in my best interest to discuss my client list with you. Hot or not."

I reached into my purse for my wallet. I held it aloft. "I'll settle your tab for the night."

He laughed. "Aw, Ms. Izzy, people are gonna think you're sweet on me."

I looked around the bar. Other than Bruce Hamilton and Shane, who was tending bar that night, the only other person in the room was a middle-aged woman in overly tight leather pants. She rested her teased blond head on one hand and took lackadaisical stabs at the cherry in her glass with a cocktail stirrer.

Given our limited—and wasted—audience, I wasn't worried that much of Merryville would hear that I'd settled Jonnie G's bar bill.

I caught Shane's eye and nodded in Jonnie's direction, eyebrows raised in question.

"Twenty-two," he called back while he slopped a dripping bar rag across the pitted surface of the bar.

I looked up at the whiteboard above the liquor bottles. Jonnie must have been drinking imports. I reached into my wallet and pulled out a ten and a twenty and slapped them on the bar.

"Pris Olson," I demanded.

"You know, the cops have already asked me about this."

That didn't surprise me. Jack was a good detective, and he wouldn't attempt to lock someone up for theft without consulting with the local fence.

"Did you answer their questions?"

"Well, a legalistic citizen such as myself must cooperate with the law when they come calling." He shrugged.

"Still, *they* didn't pay no bar tab," Jonnie said, his lips oozing into a sly grin.

"But I did, so what do you know?"

"Well, mebbe I have heard the name of Pris Olson. And mebbe I have heard she might be in need of services from someone like me."

"Have you actually spoken to her?"

"Mebbe."

The twinkle in his eye told me he had definitely spoken with Pris.

I felt dizzy. Maybe I'd been wrong. Maybe she'd fooled me again. Maybe Pris really was so hard up for cash that she'd stolen the jeweled collar dangle.

"What the cops didn't ask," Jonnie continued, "was when Ms. Pris had inquired about my services."

"And when was that?" I was growing impatient with Jonnie G's cat-and-mouse game. He knew something, and I wanted him to just spit it out.

"April."

"April?" That was about the time Pamela Rawlins came to Merryville to scope it out as a possible location for the silver anniversary. It was long before the missing collar dangle had even been announced. Pris couldn't have come looking for Jonnie G to get rid of the real prize jewels before the prize had been designed.

"What was she trying to get rid of?"

"That's personal. I wouldn't be much of a businessman if I devolved that kind of information. But it was stuff I could help her move."

I had a sudden flashback to Pris touching her pearls and then recoiling as though she'd been scalded. I'd never owned pearls—they're not really my style—but I'd heard you could tell by touch whether they were real or not. Maybe Pris was harder up than she'd let on even to me and she'd hawked her jewelry.

But it was stuff I could help her move. The import of Jonnie's words struck me.

"Meaning there's stuff you can't help people move?"

He grinned at me. "I can help just about anybody. But some transactions require the use of more middlemen than others."

"Anything recent like that?"

"Mebbe."

It was like talking to the caterpillar in Wonderland. Only Jonnie's breath was worse.

"I might have had an inquiry a couple of nights ago. Friend-of-a-friend-of-a-friend sort of deal. But we only spoke in generalities."

"Who was it?" I held my breath, waiting for him to describe tiny Mari and her abundance of golden curls. I was not at all prepared for what he said next.

"Never met the man before. Or since. Can't say I liked him much. I don't really care for artists."

CHAPTER
Twenty

I felt ridiculous.

The M-CFO was hosting a masquerade ball in the North Woods Hotel's second ballroom. As a thank-you to Merryville for playing host to the event, the organization opened the ball up to members of the community, and many of them had come out just for the fun of dressing up and drinking champagne.

There was nothing catty about this space or this event. While crews were still disassembling all the tables and privacy screens in Ballroom One, the North Woods Hotel had scattered the floor of Ballroom Two with tables draped in white linens, chairs tied with gauzy white bows, and centerpieces of summer roses and sparkling candles. They'd turned the houselights low to create some atmosphere, and it made all the partygoers look like they were walking through an old film set.

The theme of the closing masquerade was "old Hollywood." I'm five ten and curvy, with an over-abundance of pitch-black hair. My options were limited. I'd originally thought to go as Elizabeth Taylor, but in the weeks leading up to the retreat, I'd heard tell that every Merryvillian with black hair had had the exact same idea.

Instead of adding to the herd of Liz Taylors, I'd let Lucy talk me into attending the party as Sophia Loren. She'd come by my apartment that evening and decked me out in a low-cut peasant shirt and tiered skirt that she had used as a pirate lass costume a few Halloweens before. With a heavy heart-shaped locket Dru had found at a thrift store and my hair piled in soft curls on top of my head, I looked as much like Sophia Loren as a pale, green-eyed Irish girl could look.

Only problem? I was no bombshell. I couldn't muster the necessary swagger. And though Aunt Dolly and Lucy wouldn't have thought twice about showing so much bosom, I trembled in fear of a wardrobe malfunction. Besides, I could barely see through the haze of eyeliner they'd plastered on my face.

I took a sip of chardonnay and tried to discreetly hike up the neckline of my shirt.

"Stop futzing with your costume," Rena said. "Lucy

did a great job and you're going to soccer-mom it all to pieces."

"Yeah. Where's the fun in that?" Just the sound of Jack's voice made me go hot all over, but having him peering down my cleavage made my face flame.

"You snuck up on me," I complained.

He raised his eyebrows in wide-eyed innocence and took another pull from the hollow stirrer in his plastic cup of pop. "I'm the police," he mumbled around the straw. "I was surveilling."

Rena laughed. "Surveilling what?"

Jack bobbled his eyebrows. "Top secret stuff."

"You're not in costume," I said, reaching up to straighten the knot of his black tie and brush the shoulders of his charcoal suit.

"Sure I am," he said. "I'm Charlton Heston."

I stopped with my hands hovering over his shoulders. He was right. His hair was a little lighter, his eyes not so brooding, but he was otherwise a dead ringer for a young Heston.

Rena laughed again. "At least you didn't dress like Moses."

"Or Ben-Hur," Jack agreed. "It's a little drafty in here."

I couldn't suppress the smile that spread across my face, listening to two of my favorite people bantering so naturally. It was ironic, too, that the straitlaced cop should have such a rapport with my best friend. Normally, Rena's choice in wardrobe, hair color, and attitude made Merryvillians dismiss her as another degenerate from the wrong side of the tracks. Some people even thought Rena practiced witchcraft. She might curse her enemies—both real and perceived—to kingdom come, but I'd never once seen her cast a spell. But Jack saw past all of that to the sweet and loyal girl she really was.

Tonight she was dressed as Charlie Chaplin's Tramp: a three-piece suit, a tall bowler, a walking stick, lots of black eyeliner, a black felt Hitler mustache . . . and newly dyed black hair to complete the look. Jolly was feeling a little under the weather that night, so Rena had talked Sean into coming along as her plus one. He'd donned a seersucker suit and made a darned fine Atticus Finch.

Lucy had had a date with Xander (who was not keen on dressing up), but she'd helped Dru dress up like a very tall Dorothy, complete with a blue gingham dress and glittered red flats sparkling on her feet. Lucy had insisted on being faithful to the original, so she'd forced Dru to borrow my Packer to serve as her Toto, complete with tiny wicker basket. He wiggled this way and that, trying to take in the sights from his precarious perch in the basket.

I'd brought Packer's leash as a backup plan, as I couldn't see Packer putting up with being toted around in a basket for very long.

"Izzy, your dog weighs a ton."

"Oh, hush. He's not fat."

Jack sputtered a laugh. "With all the table scraps you feed that dog, it's a wonder he isn't spherical."

Everyone chuckled, and even Packer rocked from haunch to haunch, his big doggy grin wide at being the center of attention.

"You shouldn't feed the dog scraps," Sean said, his voice hard-edged. "It's not good for him."

"I know that," I said, trying not to get defensive, "but it makes him happy."

"Come on, Izzy," he snapped. "You know how this goes. He's a dog. He doesn't have judgment. You do. Use it."

Rena and Dru both gasped, and Jack took a step like he was going to angle in between me and Sean. I didn't like the look on his face.

"Sean Tucker. Can I have a word with you?"

"Of course, Izzy McHale. I'm delighted to be at your beck and call."

"Oh, stuff it, Sean."

I turned and stalked off. Out of the corner of my eye I could see Jack start to follow me, but Rena put a restraining hand on his arm.

I wasn't sure Sean was behind me until he reached ahead of me to open the ballroom door for me. I didn't look at him, but from that point forward, I could feel his presence as he followed me down the hall to a small meeting room that looked out over the hotel's lovely green space.

I took a deep breath and turned around to face Sean, intent on finally having it out with him once and for all.

Lightning flashed outside, and in the breathless moment that followed, before the grounded rumble of the thunder, Sean and I glared at each other. He took a step in my direction and I in his. Whatever had been brewing between us crackled and hissed in the half-light.

"What is going on with you?" I snapped.

"What do you mean?"

"You've been so prickly lately."

He stared at me hard, and I was reminded of the serious boy he had been. He'd always had a quick smile and a joyous laugh, but with something deeper moving in his eyes. Thoughts he rarely shared.

"I don't know," he finally replied.

I held my breath, gathering courage to ask the question that had been niggling at the back of my mind since the very first time Jack Collins kissed me.

"Is it Jack?"

"What about Jack?"

"You know."

"Are you asking if I'm jealous?"

Despite the stormy dark, I felt like I'd been staring

into the summer sun: face hot, eyes unfocused, body lethargic.

"Maybe," I conceded.

In a heartbeat, his glare softened, and his mouth lifted in a boyish half smile. "Fair question. If you'd asked me even a week ago, I might have said yes. I might have grabbed you by the shoulders and kissed you silly. I might have meant it."

I was keenly aware of how close we stood to each other. If I raised my hand just a few inches, it would brush his.

"And now?" I murmured.

"Now I think the answer is no. I'm not jealous. When we first started spending time together last fall, a part of me thought . . . well, that I would feel the same way about you. The way I felt in high school. But now I realize that we've both changed."

I wasn't so sure I'd changed. Or that he'd changed. But I kept my mouth shut.

"Back then everything was so raw," he continued. "Not just between us, but everything. I burned for you, Izzy, a passion that was out of proportion with the rest of my life. I'll never feel that ache again . . . not even for you. The night after the murder, when you kissed me in your kitchen, there was no heat to it. No heat from you or from me. Just a memory of something long gone. It's a powerful memory, but still a memory."

I won't lie. His words made me a little sad. It's like Ruth had said. There are secrets and there are secrets. Just because we both knew that the romance—even the possibility of romance—was gone from our relationship, keeping it quiet allowed us both to avoid mourning what we'd shared. Now the words were out. Spoken. Real. There was no avoiding them anymore, and we were left with no choice but to confront our loss and put it to bed.

I was scared, deep down, that this would sever the tenuous thread between us and a lifetime of love would end. I needed Sean to love me—not the way Jack loved me but the way I loved Sean and Rena and my sisters. That kind of love was no consolation prize. It was just as important a part of my life as the romantic love Jack and I shared.

As if he could read my mind, he reached out to take my hand. "I do still love you, Izzy McHale. Always will. But that love I had for you in high school, when I stood under your window and begged you to leave Casey, that was the basis for a wild romance. Not the basis of a life together."

I realized the truth in his words. Back then, if I'd let myself see past the sparkling future I'd mapped out with Casey, I might have returned Sean's love. With the benefit of hindsight, I *know* I would have. We would have had one of those wild affairs fueled by hormones and the invincibility of youth. And—who knows?—perhaps that would have settled into something more stable. Permanent. But the moment had passed, and no matter how tempting, you cannot unravel the fabric of time.

And, frankly, given how deeply I'd come to love Jack—despite my continuing inability to say the words—I wouldn't want to unroll time. Yes, the time with Casey had been hollow, but it had put me in a position to meet Jack, and I couldn't regret anything that brought me to that point.

I stepped away. Just a step, but it felt as though it ripped apart the intimacy of our conversation. The lingering tension between us drained away into the space I'd created.

"So if you're not jealous of Jack, why have you had your back up every time I've spoken with you?"

"Have I been that bad?"

"Pretty bad," I said.

He laughed. "I'm sorry. I only came to the realization that I had to let you go recently, and my heart hasn't taken the news well. It should have been the obvious conclusion the first moment I saw you look at him like he was some sort of superhero, but it didn't strike me all at once. It came in waves: first I realized that I wasn't good for you; then I realized that Jack was. In the middle there, I wasn't really myself."

"You think Jack's good for me?" Part of me knew it was strange to ask this of a man who'd professed feelings for me, but Sean had been my friend for longer than he'd been a potential love interest. His opinion mattered to me.

He nodded, and I let out a breath I hadn't realized I'd been holding. Lightning lit up the room and I could see the sincerity in his expression. "Jack's a good man, with a sense of humor and a kind heart, and he's clearly head over heels for you. He's solid. And me? I'm not quite done searching yet."

"What are you searching *for*?"

"If I knew that, I'd have found it by now. In the meantime, I have the best friends a man could hope to have. Crazy-making, but still amazing." I started to open my mouth, but he raised a hand to forestall me. "Before you ask, the answer is yes. We are most definitely still friends. You don't get to weasel out of my life quite that easily."

Another crash of thunder rattled the windows in their panes.

Without thought, I threw my arms around Sean. "Why would I ever leave you?"

"That's a good question."

The bluster of the storm had drowned out the sound of the door squealing on its hinges as it opened, and I hadn't heard Jack coming into the room, but now—with my arms still around Sean's waist and my easily misinterpreted words still hanging in the air—I couldn't focus on anything but him.

He stood like a fighter, feet braced apart, hands hanging at his sides, loose but ready to react. He must have gone outside to look for us. Rivulets of water slid down his cheeks and spilled from the folds in his jacket, but he made no move to shake off the wet. Still. He stood so still.

I couldn't read any emotion on his face, but he couldn't hide the pain in his eyes as he fixed his gaze on me.

Tension thrummed in the air like the storm's static, paralyzing me. Sean was the one who slipped out of my grip—our embrace—and stepped away. His hands raised, he said, "Everything's cool, Jack. Take care of her."

I'm not sure if Jack heard Sean or not. His full attention rested squarely on me.

I didn't break eye contact with Jack, but I was vaguely aware of Sean wrapping his jacket around his shoulders and slipping out the door.

"It's not what it looked like," I finally murmured.

"Really?"

In three long strides, Jack was at my side. He smelled good, like ozone, newly mown grass, and a hint of something darker.

I'd seen Jack serious, mostly when he was busy being Jack-the-cop. I'd seen him tender, when he brushed my hair from my face or when he lent his arm to his elderly mother. I'd seen him amused, teasing, laughing . . . all as we danced the intricate dance of flirtation. But I'd never seen Jack like this. A man, guarded, wounded, yet still somehow bold.

I didn't quite know how to approach this Jack. But honesty hadn't failed me yet.

"We're friends. Nothing more," I said.

He grunted.

"Really. Once upon a time we might have had something else, but it's gone. He likes you. Thinks you're good for me."

"I don't give a flip what Sean Tucker thinks of me. What do you think?"

I felt like we were balanced on a fulcrum. One misstep from either of us, and the surface that held us suspended in the night would crash to the ground, smashing us both with its simple gravity.

"Jack. I think you are a good, strong man. I think you make me smile at the most outrageous moments. I think you keep me from falling too far into myself, taking myself too seriously." My balance tottered, and I took a breath to steady myself. "And I think I love you."

A flash of lightning—gentler this time, as though the storm was finally moving away—illuminated Jack's face. The raindrops caught in his lashes glittered, and he swiped an arm across his face to clear them away. I searched his face for signs of a reaction, but he remained stoic.

"Seriously. Sean has moved on. He's not interested in me that way anymore. And I'm not interested in him that way either. We both thought—I don't know—that maybe we could have that magic back. The magic of being teenagers. But we can't, and frankly, now I don't even want to."

"Hush."

"Excuse me?"

"I said, hush. You really do talk a lot."

"Well, I'm pouring my heart out to you, and you're just standing there. Didn't you hear me? I think I love you."

A flicker of amusement lit up Jack's eyes, and for a second it looked like he was fighting a smile. "Think?"

I raised my hands to his chest to give him a gentle shove backward. "Okay. I know. I know I love you. You're making this hard."

He caught my hands in his and held them trapped against the heat of his body. "No. This couldn't be any easier," he said.

With the tiniest tug, he pulled me into his arms and kissed me senseless.

I let myself lean into his embrace for a moment before kissing him back, trying to convey a promise to him. A promise that I didn't just *think* I loved him but that I *knew* I loved him. That Sean's friendship was no threat to him. That the bond between us was real.

He slipped the sleeve of my peasant blouse down

to expose my shoulder and planted a hot kiss there. The angle of his head allowed the velvety brush of his hair to caress my cheek, tickling my nose with the crisp scent of his shampoo.

Lightning flashed, and I startled, but he shushed me by placing a finger to my mouth and then his lips on mine. At that point, the entirety of the outside world disappeared. Jack consumed every one of my senses.

I don't know how long we stood there, each caught in the orbit of the other, but finally I pulled away. My movement caught him off-balance as he continued to follow my mouth with his. I giggled, and he chuckled in response. I could feel the laughter in his body more than I heard it, and I couldn't wipe the smile off my face.

"Jack," I chided softly, "this is delightful, but I have to tell you something."

He sobered instantly, pulled back. "What?" he asked, wariness deepening his voice.

"Don't get all bristly on me. I think I know who really killed Phillip Denford."

CHAPTER
Twenty-one

"I don't know how I feel about this," Jack muttered.

"I do. You hate it."

"You're right. I hate it. On many levels."

I laughed, but threw my arms around him to give him a placating hug. "It will be all right. You know we won't get a confession if you're in the room, and I'm the perfect bait for our suspect."

"Bait? I really don't like the sound of that."

"You're going to be right on the other side of the door, and Xander has worked his electronics magic so you'll be able to see and hear everything my phone picks up as it is happening."

Jack frowned. "We should have backup."

"You're all the backup I need, baby."

He kissed me hard, then let me go. We had a killer to catch.

"So tell me more about this dot-com thing," I shouted.

"Now? Here?" The ballroom was thumping with the bass of some 1980s techno band, and I could barely hear him above the people packed in close around us. I couldn't hear him, but I could certainly see him. He wore an elaborate costume, Rudolph Valentino in *The Sheik*, and he leaned in so close I could feel the heat from his body and smell the musk of his cologne.

I wasn't proud of it then and I'll never be proud of it in the future, but I leaned forward just enough that my low-cut peasant shirt showed a bit of cleavage. "How about the hotel bar?" I suggested.

I'd wanted to get a room, someplace really private where I knew I could get Peter to let his guard down, but Jack had put the kibosh on that immediately. The hotel bar had been our compromise. With the hotel filled with cat fanciers who were all attending the masquerade ball, the bar was nigh on empty, and the instrumental soft rock they played over their speakers wouldn't interfere with the sound from my phone.

As expected, Peter glanced down at my cleavage before his eyes bounced right back to mine. He looked confused for an instant, then shrugged. "Sure."

I led him away from the raucous ballroom, down a dimly lit corridor to the hotel's Aurora Bar. The bar could have been in any hotel in Middle America. The only thing that set it apart at all was the swoosh of green, blue, and purple neon lights, which were meant to mimic the aurora borealis.

I ordered Peter a gin and tonic and got myself a glass of pop. We took a seat in a high-backed booth set away from the bar.

"So the thing with theartisanway.com is that people will simply stumble over you there. For your Web site, someone has to be searching for pet clothes or something similar to find you, but if you're on Artisan, people who are just generally browsing homemade goods might see your store. Or maybe you'll be featured on the main page someday."

"Mmm-hmm. Listen. I don't really want to talk about theartisanway.com. Though I do appreciate the tip. It sounds great."

"Then why . . .? Oh." He smiled a sultry bedroom smile and nudged his glass forward with one knuckle until it clinked against mine. "I have to admit I'm flattered, but I'm with someone else now. Once upon a time, I would have taken you up on your offer, though. You *are* hot."

"Get over yourself, Peter. I'm not the least bit interested in you. I don't just fall into bed when a pretty boy with a daddy complex gives me a little wink. Though it's nice to know I'm hot."

"Then why . . . ?"

"I don't think you're getting it," I said, trying to keep my tone as businesslike as possible, given our setting and my ridiculous getup. "I know what you did."

"You've lost me," he said, but there was a note of trepidation in his voice.

"For instance, I know you stole the jeweled collar dangle."

He narrowed his eyes. "What makes you think that?"

"Because I talked to a fence down at the Silent Woman. I know you were at the bar, because you got yourself thrown out. And Jonnie G says you approached him about moving some big stones."

"I don't know any Jonnie G. I was drunk out of my mind that night at the bar."

I shook my head. "Well, you may not remember him, but he sure remembers you. You were talking business and then you hit on his girl. He described you to a tee and even knew that you were an artist."

"Okay. First of all, I wasn't hitting on his girl. I was making friendly conversation. Like I said, I'm involved with someone else. Besides, so I talked to some guy when I was drunk. That doesn't mean a thing."

"It does when you add it to the fact that the dangle that rolled out of Pris Olson's bag was a fake."

"Do tell."

"Jolly said she always solders her jump rings together so the real dangle would have had limited movement in its cage. It should have been nearly silent as it rolled. But I could hear the fake one clanking as it rolled from clear across the room. It must have gotten knocked loose from the jump ring so it was freely tumbling against the sides of the cage, something that couldn't have happened if the ring had been soldered together. In fact, when the little cage came to a rest, the dangle was lying flat on the bottom as though it weren't attached to the cage anymore at all. The dangle that was stolen that day was a forgery, because the real one—with the genuine gems—had already been taken."

"That doesn't mean that I'm the one who took it."

"It had to be you. Before the show, the only people who had even seen the design for the dangle were you, your father, and Jolly Nielson. You're the only person involved who had the pattern and the skills to make such a perfect replica. But you knew that when the show was over and someone actually won the thing, they'd get a new appraisal and the forgery would be caught. You had to steal the fake one, too."

"I don't understand what you want me to say," Peter said.

"I want you to admit what you did. Planting the dangle in Pris's bag was brilliant. You knew she had financial troubles, so people would believe she was a thief if they found her in possession of the dangle. But you also knew that if she simply found the thing in her purse later that night, she couldn't go to the cops without looking like a suspect."

I cocked my head to one side. "It was really rather genius."

"It doesn't make any sense. Let's say, hypothetically, that I stole the original dangle and replaced it with a fake. I couldn't have stolen the fake. I saw you not long after the lights came on. You saw that I was kitty-corner across the room from Pris's stall. How did I get out to darken the lights and then get back in, steal the dangle, get to Pris's stall, plant the dangle, and then get clear to the other side of the room . . . all while still holding the cup of coffee you said I abandoned on the table? I never leave a cup of coffee half-drunk. That's stuff's my lifeblood."

He was right. He'd still had his coffee in his hand after the lights went out. And the day the cat fanciers came out to Red, White & Bleu for lunch, he'd taken his coffee black, but the coffee I'd thrown away that day was pale with cream or milk.

And it had smelled like Taffy's Happy Leaf Tea Shoppe. Like flowers.

Like lavender.

Suddenly the pieces fell into place. We'd had such a hard time figuring out who'd done it because we'd been looking for one person . . . when it was actually two.

Peter would have had to have help in order to steal the collar ornament: one person to turn out the lights, one person to steal the dangle. And Peter never got close enough to Pris or her station to dump the dangle in her purse, but Peter's partner had. Marsha Denford.

I remembered it as clear as day then. First the brush of someone moving past me during the blackout: Peter moving to the corner from which he eventually joined our little group. Then Peter and Marsha clasping hands and Marsha turning to pull a startled Pris into her arms. The transfer of the collar dangle from one person to the next went off without a hitch.

But why would Marsha have helped Peter steal the counterfeit collar dangle?

For the same reason Mari fell all over Phillip and Marsha and Pamela couldn't stand the sight of each other. They were in love.

It's in the blood. Like father, like son. Marsha and Peter hadn't had a mother-son relationship at all. They were virtually peers, tied together by their need for Phillip's money. It was natural that their common situation would drive them into each other's arms.

"Next I suppose you're going to accuse me of killing my father," he said with a smug smile.

"Actually, yes." I straightened in my seat. I was starting to doubt that I'd get him to admit to anything.

"Someone was driving Phillip around town the morning he died, and I know you did that."

"Everyone drove my father around. He lost his license years ago, after a string of unfortunate DUIs."

"Right, but Marsha isn't one to play the errand boy, and Mari was sick that morning. She wouldn't have wanted to be in a moving car. It had to be you."

"I still don't see how this adds up to murder."

"Did he catch you?" I asked.

"What?"

"Did Phillip catch you and Marsha together in the ballroom that morning? Is that why you killed him?"

He didn't respond.

"Look, between my statement and the physical evidence, the police have all the pieces already. They've got the forged collar dangle, which is sure to have your prints on it. Someone at Joe Time surely saw you that morning, ordering a black coffee for yourself and a lavender latte for Marsha. They'll surely pull prints from the piece of wood used to beat poor Ruth to death. The pieces are all there, Peter. It's just a question of putting them together, and they'll do that eventually."

He sighed and looked up, over my shoulder. I glanced back and saw that Jack had made his presence known.

"It was my idea." Peter sighed. "Let's be perfectly straight. I love Marsha, and I won't see her go to jail for my crimes."

"Tell me about it," I said, leaning forward and raising a hand to warn Jack from coming closer.

"It was my idea to replace the stupid cat collar with a fake and hawk the real gems. You know how much my father spent on that thing? Nearly a hundred thousand dollars for something a dang cat would wear on its collar. It was obscene. All that money that he got by stealing other people's dreams, and then he wouldn't spend even a few thousand to help me get my art degree, help me get a show in Minneapolis, or even help my buddies and me set up theartisanway. com. Instead, he spent all that money—which could have launched my career ten times over—on a piece of jewelry for a cat.

"So I decided to steal the gems so I could start the Web site. My father didn't know it, but he was my secret investor. I needed the money to put out the call for artists, to drive traffic to the site, to make sure the site looked as high-end as it should. I just needed to get my foot in the door.

"I stole the original, but then I realized I'd eventually have to steal the fake, too, so no one would know it was a forgery. I didn't want to get Marsha involved, but she knew how dire my circumstances were and she offered to help. All Marsha did was turn off the lights. Then, later, after the hubbub over the dangle going missing had died down a bit and everyone was focused on my father's death, I passed it to her so she could drop the bauble in Pris's bag."

I remembered the dance they had done, Peter embracing Marsha and clasping her hands so tightly—

around the dangle, as it turned out—and then Marsha pulling Pris into an unexpected hug, the perfect time to drop the dangle in Pris's big shoulder tote.

"So Marsha helped a little with the theft, but the murder was all me."

"Why did you kill your dad?"

"You know. He was supposed to go up to get changed after I brought him back to the hotel, but he didn't have his room key on him. For a savvy man, he was helpless. Marsha and Mari managed everything for him. I don't think he even knew how to use an ATM. So he came into the ballroom, looking for Marsha, and found us together. Just holding hands, but he knew. He'd been suspicious for months. He threatened to divorce Marsha and disinherit me. After all those years I was his toady, he was going to leave me with nothing. I grabbed the shears from Ruth's station and stabbed him."

"What did Marsha do?"

"She took the rest of Ruth's grooming kit and got rid of it. I don't even know why. There were so many pairs of shears in that room, what did it matter where they came from?"

"I don't know."

"Turns out it was a really bad idea. Ruth suspected that her shears were the murder weapon, and while you were asking questions, she was, too. She got too close. She actually followed Marsha when she slipped away for one of her regular afternoon 'naps' and saw me open my hotel room door to let Marsha in. Thankfully, I spotted Ruth ducking behind a room-service tray. It was only a matter of time before she put all the pieces together and realized what happened, especially if she compared notes with you. When I heard her telling T. J. Leuzinger that she was going to meet you out by the agility course, I followed her. She looked me dead in the eye and said, 'I know what you did.' I didn't even think. I just picked up the closest object—part of the hurdle—and swung at her. When I realized she was dead, I stuffed her in the tube to buy myself time to slip back into the crowd and disappear."

That was what stung the most. I would never wish anyone dead, but if ever there was a man who needed killing, it was Phillip Denford. Ruth Kimmey, though, was innocent of every crime, save curiosity—something I could hardly fault her for. To think that one man's greed could lead to so much pain made me especially grateful for all the generous people in my life.

CHAPTER
Twenty-two

Despite my best efforts to be upbeat, my farewell to Ingrid and Harvey the next day was more bitter than sweet. The whole gang gathered at Trendy Tails for a bon-voyage party, complete with streamers, balloons, and a cake, but the festivities felt forced. We had already resigned ourselves to seeing less of Ingrid and Harvey when they'd originally planned to split their time between Merryville and Boca. And this wasn't goodbye forever, as we all had an open invitation to go visit them whenever we wanted—even Packer and Jinx. But it still felt so final.

Dolly and Richard sat hand in hand, their public display of affection a clear sign of how hard hit they both were at the thought of Ingrid and Harvey leaving for good. Even Dolly's wardrobe was solemn . . .

for Dolly. She wore her favorite tangerine platform sandals but paired them with a pair of hot-pink capris and a hot-pink T-shirt that boasted only a smattering of sequins.

Rena ate a bowl of ice cream with less enthusiasm than I've ever in my life seen someone eat a bowl of ice cream, while Sean stood with his arm draped around her shoulders. He stared at the floor, his dark runaway curls obscuring almost all of his face.

My mom, Lucy, and Dru were huddled together in a little knot of mourning. I actually heard my mother sniff. I was so close with Ingrid that I'd forgotten Ingrid and my mother had a much longer relationship, more a bonding of peers than a mentor-mentee relationship.

For my part, I sat next to Jack, trying to make conversation, with Jinx draped over my lap and Packer sleeping in a tight circle beneath my chair.

"So how did you figure out it wasn't Pris?" Ingrid asked.

"All along it just didn't seem like the sort of crime she'd commit. The evidence against her kept mounting: she'd changed her clothes the morning of the murder. She'd been in possession of the dangle, been to see a fence. But it always felt a little off. When I went to see Pris before the masquerade, I just flat-out asked her about her change of wardrobe that morning. Where was she and why wouldn't she tell the police about an alibi if she had one?"

"And?"

"She was seeing a divorce lawyer."

"Really? But she's stuck with that sleazeball Hal for so many years."

"Right. Because if she walked away, she got nothing. But they were broke. The day before, Phillip had said he was going to force Hal out of the development and Pris had had to fend off a call from Sandra Lowe, the woman who moved her family to Merryville to live in one of the imaginary condos. At that point she figured that even if she got everything Hal had, she'd have a big fat goose egg. There was absolutely no reason for her to stick with him."

"But why not tell the cops?" Jack asked. "That alibi would have gone a long way to clearing her of the theft, and Gil Dixon was pretty certain that the two crimes—the theft and the murder—were related."

"She didn't want anyone to know. By the time she got back from the lawyer and changed into more appropriate clothes for the long day of work ahead of her, Phillip was dead and the Olsons' financial situation was on the upswing again. She didn't want Hal to know she'd gone to see an attorney, for fear it would prompt him to do the same."

"People are so complicated," Ingrid said.

"Aren't they?" I tried to lighten the mood a little. "Now, enough of all this glum talk. Harvey, I can't wait to meet your daughter and your grandkids."

"Oh, yeah." The reticent Harvey smiled. "You'll love my Julie. You two are a lot alike."

Ingrid huffed. "Julie doesn't get in nearly as much trouble as Izzy here."

"Amen to that," Jack offered.

"I don't get into trouble alone, you know. Everyone in this room has played some role in getting me into some sort of mess."

"That's what friends are for," Sean offered with a small grin. "Getting you into trouble."

"And, to be fair," Dru chimed in, "we've all had a hand in getting you out of those messes, too."

"Also what friends are for," Sean said.

"Well, then, by golly, I'm blessed with some of the best friends a girl could have." My eyes flew to Ingrid's face, and I choked on the last word.

"Oh my heavens," Ingrid said. "What a bunch of Gloomy Gusses you all are! We're not dying. We're moving to Florida."

"Same difference," Lucy said, a hint of her snarky self peeking through the gloom.

"Young lady, you have no idea what we do in our village. We play badminton and tennis and croquet and bocce. We have speaker events. Do you know how many visits from presidential candidates the community received in the last election? You'd think that residents of Shady Creeks were the only voters in America. Heck, we've even got a disco on-site."

The image of Ingrid and Harvey doing the hustle beneath a disco ball broke the tension and we were all finally able to laugh.

Ingrid drew herself up even straighter in her seat, head high. "In case you didn't already know, I'm giving the house to Izzy. She can keep running Trendy Tails here or do whatever she wants with it. I would just note," she added, looking pointedly at Jack, "that there are a lot of bedrooms in this house."

Harvey patted her on the arm. "Ingrid, darling, don't make the boy blush."

Jack had, indeed, gotten some color in his cheeks, and I couldn't help but grin. Ingrid had never had children, which meant she'd never had grandchildren, and she was eager for someone to spoil.

"So what are you planning to do with the business?" Jack asked, deftly changing the subject. "Since Phillip is himself no longer a threat, are you going to take a wait-and-see approach?"

Rena chimed in. "No way. First of all, Phillip's company survives him, and we have no idea whether they'll decide to run with his idea. Either way, though, this experience has made us very aware of how tenuous our situation is. We do great with locals and tourists, but if we want to grow—and we *need* to grow—we'll be doing it online, where we're competing in a crowded industry."

Sean laughed. "You sound like a regular tycoon. I'd

never in a million years have expected to hear you talking about business with such ease."

"Well, I mostly like to bake dog biscuits, but I'll learn whatever I have to learn to be able to keep on doing that."

I leaned forward. "We've decided to do a little re-branding. We'll work up to a launch of a new store called Swag and Wags. We'll emphasize that our garments are bespoke, made by hand to the exact measurements of your pet. And we'll offer a limited selection of human clothes to match our pet collections. We think that will carve us a nice niche in the industry."

Ingrid beamed. "I'm so proud of you two. You're going to take the business world by storm, and I can't wait to watch."

"By the way, what happened with Peter and Marsha Denford?" Dru asked.

"They were both booked for conspiracy to commit grand larceny and murder two," Jack answered. "While Peter won't say another word, Marsha is singing like Streisand. I'd say she's within an inch of a deal, and then the weight of the offenses will fall on Peter."

"I have to admit, what they did was absolutely horrible, but I thought it was kind of sweet the way Peter rolled over when it looked like Marsha would be implicated, making sure to downplay her role. For him, it's true love," I said.

"You. Are. Such. A. Sap," Lucy said with a waggle of her head.

"I'm not the one who was writing 'I heart Xander' and 'Lucy Stephens' all over the scratch paper at the front of the store."

"They were just doodles."

"Girls!" my mother snapped. "I've raised all three of you—"

" 'Three of you'? How did I get dragged into this?" Dru whined.

"Nothing, dear," my mom replied, as Lucy and I mouthed "Nothing, dear" in sync. My mother was always placating Dru, assuring her she wasn't a derelict like Lucy and me.

"Jeez, Dru," Dolly groused. "You're never any fun."

Sean nodded in Jack's direction. "You sure you want a part of this?"

Jack laughed. "Sometimes I fear for my life when they form a pack like this, but in ones and twos, I can hold my own against the McHale women."

"As I was saying," my mom continued pointedly, "I raised all three of you girls, and you all have tender hearts. Which is why, young man," she said, turning on Jack, "if you hurt my girl, all the McHale women—"

"And me!"

"Me too!"

"Me three!"

"—all the McHale women and Dolly, Ingrid, and Rena will give you no peace."

Jack looked at Sean, and Sean offered a wry smile and a shrug in response.

"I wouldn't dare hurt Izzy," Jack said softly, staring down at me as I gazed up into his handsome face. "In fact, I've got a proposition."

He leaned down to lift Jinx off my lap and drape the cat over his own shoulder. "Jinx," he said in a stage whisper, "I know this cat named Steve, and he's a fine fellow. How would you feel about having him as a roommate?"

"That girl's not going to give her cat to you, son," Richard Greene said.

"Oh, hush, Dickie. Jack's asking Izzy to move in with him."

"Well, he's not doing a very good job of it," Richard said.

A chorus of "Hush" rang out in the room.

"Actually, Richard's right. I'm mucking this up." Jack carefully set Jinx on the floor and dropped to a knee. "Izzy McHale, I'm not asking you to move in with me. I'm asking you to marry me."

I gasped.

"I know this isn't the most romantic time or place, and I don't even have a ring. But standing here in the warm circle of your friends and family, basking in the generosity of your spirit, listening to you empathize with a criminal and say goodbye to one of your dearest friends, I just see you. I see years of Christmases and birthdays and Sunday family dinners. And I see years of simply being by your side as you go about your wacky way, occasionally stepping in to keep you from harm's way."

I felt the tears welling in my eyes.

"I know it's sudden, but happiness is a sudden feeling. You make me happy, Izzy, and you already know how much I love you. Be my wife?"

I took a moment to scan the faces of my friends and family, and I saw nothing there but encouragement. Or perhaps I was simply projecting my own emotion onto them. Either way, their support reaffirmed what I knew in my heart: that Jack Collins was the man for me.

I slid off my chair so that I was kneeling next to him. I'm sure we looked ridiculous, especially with Packer jumping about and wriggling, trying to get between us. But I just didn't care.

"Jack Collins," I whispered, "let's get hitched."

RECIPES

Portobello Tacos with Roasted Pepper and Tomatillo Salsa

Ingredients

  4 portobello mushroom caps, stemmed, degilled,
     and sliced into wide pieces, marinated
  Refried beans (canned is fine)
  Fresh flour tortillas
  Grape tomatoes
  Cheddar or Mexican cheese, grated
  Sour cream
  Tomatillo and roasted pepper salsa

Marinade

  ¼ c. oil
  3 Tbs. orange juice

3 Tbs. lime juice
2 Tbs. tequila
1 tsp. chili powder
1 tsp. kosher salt
1 tsp. sugar
½ tsp. liquid smoke

Combine all of the marinade ingredients in a bowl, toss with the sliced mushrooms. Cover and allow to marinate at room temperature for about an hour. Heat a skillet over medium-high heat. Using a slotted spoon, transfer mushrooms to the skillet and cook, stirring occasionally, until the mushrooms are nicely browned. Meanwhile, heat beans in a small saucepan over medium-low heat. Heat tortillas in the oven or toaster oven until just warm. Create tacos by spreading a spoonful of beans on a tortilla. Top with some sliced mushroom, cheese, tomatoes, sour cream, and a dollop of the brilliant salsa.

Tomatillo Salsa

6 poblano peppers
10 tomatillos, husked and rinsed, patted dry
large bunch of cilantro leaves (¾ c.)
lime juice to taste (probably ¼ c.)
1 heaping Tbs. minced garlic
5–6 green onions, white and light green parts only

1 tsp. kosher salt
½ tsp. sugar

Preheat broiler. Put tomatillos and peppers on a baking sheet and broil until starting to blacken (about 5 minutes per side). Put peppers in a large bowl, cover with plastic, and let steam about 10 minutes. Meanwhile coarsely chop green onions, garlic, cilantro, and tomatillos. Remove peppers and destem, peel, remove seeds, and coarsely chop. Add to the other ingredients, then throw in the salt and sugar. Pulse in a food processor until blended but not pureed.

About the Author

Annie Knox is the national bestselling author of the Pet Boutique mysteries, including *Paws for Murder* and *Groomed for Murder*. She doesn't commit—or solve—murders in her real life, but her passion for animals is one hundred percent true. She's also a devotee of eighties music, Asian horror films, and reality TV. While Annie is a native Buckeye and has called a half-dozen states home, she and her husband now live a stone's throw from the courthouse square in a north Texas town in their very own crumbling historic house.

Also available from
national bestselling author
Annie Knox

Paws for Murder
A Pet Boutique Mystery

Izzy McHale wants her new Trendy Tails Pet
Boutique in Merryville, Minnesota, to be the
height of canine couture and feline fashions. But
at the store's opening, it turns out it's a human
who's dressed to kill....

**"I'm already panting for the next book in
the series."**
—*New York Times* bestselling author
Miranda James

"Five paws up!"
—**Melissa Bourbon, author of**
A Killing Notion

Available wherever books are sold or at
penguin.com

facebook.com/TheCrimeSceneBooks

OM0139